"I liked you that first date," Frankie said.

"I wasn't supposed to, and then when we went geocaching and you touched me, I—" She looked at Decker, running a hand over his cheek. "I wanted places that were the opposite of sexy. I wanted distance."

"There is no distance now." His husky tone spun into the evening and his soul sang as her fingers stroked his face.

"Nope. So there really is only one question." She raised a brow.

"You going to let me in on it?" His fingers ran along her waist. He caught every single hitch of her breath. She was driving him wild with the gentle strokes on his cheek, but he was affecting her, too.

"Are you going to kiss me, Decker?"

The only answer he gave was the dip of his head. Their lips connected and the noise of the London streets disappeared. This was as close to heaven as he'd ever been.

Dear Reader,

I love over-the-top love stories. Modern-day fairy tales you can get lost in. So when an idea for a matchmaker who falls for her client dropped into my head, I knew I had to give Frankie her happily-ever-after.

Frankie Archer has done it all. As she bounces from job to job, her résumé makes her look like a woman who can't make up her mind. Which isn't really the case. Frankie knows what she wants, but her family doesn't approve. So she's signed on to work for the best matchmaking firm in London, determined this is the career for her. Except falling for her first client wasn't part of the plan.

Decker Heughs made his father's dreams come true. Work is his life and he's made his jewelry firm the best in the country. But his mother's dream of seeing him with a partner who fulfills him isn't anywhere close to completion—particularly because he is his matchmaking firm's longest-running problem case. But when he's "matched" with Frankie, all that seems to change—except she's not a real date. Falling for his fake date isn't all that bad…right?

Enjoy Decker and Frankie's fairy tale!

Juliette Hyland

FALLING FOR
HIS FAKE DATE

JULIETTE HYLAND

ROMANCE

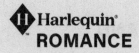

Harlequin®
ROMANCE

ISBN-13: 978-1-335-21639-7

Falling for His Fake Date

Copyright © 2025 by Juliette Hyland

Recycling programs for this product may not exist in your area.

 Harlequin Enterprises ULC
22 Adelaide St. West, 41st Floor
Toronto, Ontario M5H 4E3, Canada
www.Harlequin.com

Printed in U.S.A.

Juliette Hyland began crafting heroes and heroines in high school. She lives in Ohio with her Prince Charming, who has patiently listened to many rants regarding characters failing to follow the outline. When not working on fun and flirty happily-ever-afters, Juliette can be found spending time with her beautiful daughters and giant dogs or sewing uneven stitches with her sewing machine.

Visit the Author Profile page
at Harlequin.com for more titles.

For Gamma. You are missed beyond words.

CHAPTER ONE

FRANKIE ARCHER'S TOES screamed as she raced across the pavement. One stop for coffee shouldn't have put her behind schedule but she couldn't move as fast in the torture devices she'd strapped to her ankles this morning. Which meant she was dangerously close to arriving late on her first day at the Andilet firm.

The name felt more like a law office than the top matchmaking company for the ultra-wealthy in London. A modern-day marriage mart. Except the ton now met in private backrooms where dates were set up by well-known, but discreet, matchmakers.

Not technically marriages of convenience, but you knew the individual you'd meet for dinner was on the same social level as you. It pleased your parents or whoever was worried about the social status of the person meeting you at the altar.

Frankie's wrist buzzed and she didn't have to look at her smartwatch to know it was her older sister, Catalina. Her dad's good luck text an hour ago had simply been: Don't mess it up this time. Her mother's had reminded her that Andilet was the best place Frankie had ever worked. It was prestigious. She hadn't said she was proud of Frankie, but it was the closest Frankie had ever gotten to receiving the words.

Her sister was more diplomatic than her parents. Catalina, who, unlike Frankie, refused any shortened version of her name, was responsible for sending the "supportive" text. All members of the family played their roles and Catalina was the dutiful first-born daughter.

And I'm the daughter who can't get her life together.

Frankie didn't bother to look down to read it. She'd seen some version of each family member's text at least once or twice a year since she made the decision to skip college. Something her PhD parents and pediatrician sister couldn't fathom— particularly since she'd subsequently bounced from job to job.

It had never bothered Frankie, until she'd worked as a fashion designer's assistant. For once, she'd loved her work. She'd thought she'd finally found her dream job. She'd stayed late, helped with projects—only to be let go when the head designer discovered it was the lowly assistant's designs he was showing his best clients. Instead of a promotion, they'd shown her the door.

It was the first time she'd mourned the loss of a job. And when she'd complained to friends and family about it, they'd all laughed it off. No drinks after hours to complain about the unfairness. No sympathy flowers or cards. Just the reminder that she was the failure; couldn't even make the dream job work.

If the dream wasn't possible, then the least she could do was make her family proud. Show them she was more than a job hopper. Though her résumé disagreed. Frankie had so many different positions on there that it looked like a mishmash of roles an actress might try to claim.

Even the career counselor she'd hired had looked at her résumé with horror.

Not very professional.

But if the professionals thought it so horrid, then it was past time she stuck with something.

So today was day one of matchmaking at the top London firm. The career counselor couldn't believe she'd landed the interview, let alone the job, but Frankie was determined. She'd made sure to spin the "variety" on her résumé as life experience few others had, and pointed out few other people her age had worked in so many industries. She hadn't expected the interview strategy to work, but she'd jumped at the job offer.

Besides, matchmaking seemed fun and unique. Flyaway Frankie, the "loving" nickname her family used far too often these days, was going to make a point of staying at this job. Set down roots and grow a real career.

Her wrist buzzed again, and Frankie closed her eyes as she pressed forward. She'd send a note to Catalina on her lunch break or after the day was over. Or maybe tomorrow morning.

She opened her eyes just in time to see a man get out of a car ahead of her, staring at the phone in his hand. Which would be fine, except he was barreling toward her. Frankie tried to step around the giant, but before her brain could register too much, the man was pushing past her. Her coffee was tumbling and suddenly her already pained toes were hot.

"Ouch. Hey!"

The man turned, clearly only just now registering Frankie's existence. She'd been invisible. Not for the first time in her life but still it was hard for her confidence not to deflate a little. She was going to have to walk into work in sticky wet heels.

On her first day.

"Sorry." The man pressed bills into her hand. "I didn't mean to bump you." His dark brown gaze finally fell on her face and he paused for a second.

Maybe it was vain, but Frankie took a little pleasure in watching the heat rise in his cheeks. She'd taken time with her appearance this morning. Put a bright yellow flower in her natural brown curls to complement the yellow sundress she was wearing. Her heels—the ones she now hated—were yellow too.

"You look like sunshine." His voice was deep,

almost gravelly. The man was stunning. At least six feet. Dark black hair, a summer tan even though it was only April. "I am sorry I bumped you. If that isn't enough to cover the shoes, send a note to Heughs Jewelry."

Then he turned his attention back to the phone in his hand and walked off.

Frankie looked at her feet, then at the notes in her hand. Ten fifty-pound notes. She blinked and looked again. Nope, definitely all fifty-pound notes. Five hundred pounds, which would indeed cover the cost of her shoes, and then some. But fifty-pound notes...

Frankie had only ever seen those once. When she worked in a shop on Oxford Street. Even then, the owner had told her not to accept them as they might be counterfeit and politely informed the customer that they needed to pay with credit. Which the woman had done, though with an air of annoyance.

She pushed the bills into her purse. Right now she needed to get to work.

She walked to the front door of Andilet. It was clear from the mahogany door this was a posh place. With no nameplate you had to know what it was to find it.

She rang the bell, announced herself and waited for the quiet buzz of the lock. As she grabbed the handle, Frankie took a deep breath. Today was the first day of her career, not a job. A career.

I can do this.

"Amelia will see you in her office." Patrice, the receptionist she'd met during her interview, didn't look up from whatever was catching her attention on the screen before her.

"Thank you," Frankie muttered as she tried to pretend that getting called into the boss's office before human resources even checked you in was a good sign.

She wasn't late. She'd arrived right on time. Literally buzzing in at eight fifty-nine. She was paid from nine to five, but what if there was some unwritten rule that you arrived a half hour early?

"Francesca." Amelia Roberts stood up from her desk and gestured for Frankie to take a seat in the plush blue chair in front of it.

"Frankie. I go by Frankie." She smiled and took a seat, grateful to be off her pained feet. These shoes were not getting replaced. They were going right into the bin when she got back to her flat.

"Francesca is more elevated. And our clients expect elevation." Amelia offered a smile holding no hint of friendliness. "Andilet is the most respected luxury matchmaking service in the game. Our clients do not pay a retainer of thirty thousand pounds for cutesy nicknames, Francesca."

Frankie nodded. Less than two minutes in and she was already getting scolded over her choice of moniker. Something she felt she should have a choice of.

Silly me.

"Your first assignment is Decker Heughs." Amelia passed a tablet toward her. The dark gaze staring back at her sent shivers down her spine. The Adonis from this morning. Less than ten minutes ago he'd pressed money into her hand and strode away. Now he looked back at her from the tablet in her lap. Suddenly the instruction to contact the most exclusive jewelry company in the city made more sense.

"I see." Would Heughs remember the sunshine girl he'd passed five hundred pounds? Probably not.

Five hundred pounds was a good sum to her. To him it was like dropping a couple pounds on a cookie or some other treat. A throwaway amount.

"No. You don't." Amelia sat back in her seat, crossing her arms. "You are the newest matchmaker. Decker is the only client we can't match." She tapped her fingers on her arm as she shook her head. "I can clear everyone in sixty days or less. But this man." Amelia glared at the tablet. "For three years, this man goes on exactly three dates with anyone I set him up with and then, poof! The dates say he is *not for them.* No one complains that he's a louse. In fact they all gush that he is such a sweet man, kind, but not for them."

Panic boiled at the back of Frankie's throat. Was Amelia giving her Decker so she would fail? She'd set up exactly no one! How was she supposed to find the perfect match for the company's longest running bachelor?

"So you want me to find someone for him?" Frankie pushed past the first photo.

Hobbies: none.
Favorite food: Whatever is in the kitchen.
Favorite band: Don't really listen to music.

Gee. Why was it so difficult to figure out a mate for him?

"No." Amelia took a deep breath, then leaned forward on her elbows. "I want you to date him."

Frankie's mouth was hanging open. Words were rushing through her brain, but none of them slipped to her tongue. *Date him?*

"Are you going to say something? Or just flop your mouth there for fun?"

"I apologize, I just…" *Why am I apologizing?* This was ridiculous. Insulting. "I was under the impression that this was a matchmaking agency not an escort service." Dear God, how had she misread the hiring package?

Amelia's cheeks flamed as she grabbed a pen and notepad from her top drawer. "I do not like your insinuation."

"Sorry." Again, Frankie was issuing the apology. "I don't understand."

"Clearly." Her boss started jotting down notes on the pad. "Decker is a tough case. The man is a blank slate. I have nothing to go on and every beautiful woman I set him up with is a bust. So—" she lifted her gaze, the jewellike eyes boring directly into Frankie "—I need to find out what the man does on the third date that makes everyone walk away. And that is where you come in. You will go on three dates with him. Just three. You will report back to me about the evenings so that I can clear him from our client list."

Before Frankie could say anything, Amelia pointed a boney finger at her. "*And* you will not kiss him. You will not sleep with him. You will not demean the good name of Andilet. After this, you will start your training as a matchmaker."

Frankie knew she should stand up, toss the tablet onto Amelia's desk and storm out. Say thanks but no thanks. And she would…if her family wasn't already betting on how long this lasted. If she hadn't sworn to herself that this time was different.

The idea of walking out; proving everyone right, even when the offer was so unsettling, felt like a knife in her already-tender heart. They hadn't believed she was upset to lose the fashion job. No one would buy this story.

"When is the first date?" The words were bitter sand.

But I got them out.

"Tonight. All the details are in the cubicle Patrice will show you to. Your job today is to go through that file. Figure him out. Be his perfect date."

"I assume I'll get overtime for this?" She was not working for free. Not for anyone, and certainly not for an employer suggesting such an "adventure."

"Yes." The clipped word made it clear Amelia had hoped Frankie wouldn't ask.

Amelia brushed her hand toward the door and Frankie stood. She was dismissed. Time to learn about the man who'd overpaid for her shoes this morning.

Decker Heughs rolled his shoulders and tried to ignore his racing heartbeat. This was just a dinner date. An easy dinner date.

So were the other forty-seven.

Forty-seven! That was how many first dates Andilet had set him up with in the last three years. It had to be a record. Hell, it was probably a record several times over.

Amelia had not so smoothly asked him if he was actually serious about settling down. She'd said there was no judgment in the words, but he'd heard it all the same.

Decker was a failure at finding a mate. And the issue was his. The women he knew who'd used the agency were all partnered up now—mostly. He knew three women who'd backed out of their engagements before walking down the aisle. Did Andilet still count those "successes"? Probably.

Besides, Decker had never even gotten that far. All his matches disengaged after the third date.

Right before things might get serious. It was never dramatic. If it was, that might make him feel better. Instead, the women all said he was very nice, kind, a gentleman—just not for me.

Not for me.

What was he supposed to do with that feedback?

And it wasn't like he wasn't trying. Decker believed in love. Wanted it. He knew what life was like with it…and without it.

His father had died alone. Talking about Heughs Jewelry and a business meeting that he was definitely not going to make. It made a sad moment tragic.

On the other hand, his mother and his stepfather were still blissfully happy going into their thirty-fifth anniversary. When his mother had been diagnosed with dementia two years ago, the realization that he was going to lose her had hit hard.

As had the wistful comment that if she didn't see Decker wed in the next few years, she wouldn't remember it happening.

The off-the-cuff comment had struck straight to Decker's soul. He'd spent his whole life recreating his father's dream. Heughs Jewelry was a success again. His pieces walked red carpets, were sought-after engagement pieces and status symbols.

But his mother, his rock, the woman who'd cheered him on, while worrying he was giving himself too much to her ex-husband's dream, had only ever wanted him happy in life with a partner that made him feel as loved as Harry made her feel.

How could he deny her that?

"You going in, sir?" The driver he'd hired to take him to the fancy restaurant Andilet always used for first dates didn't look too pressed. The meter was still running, after all.

"Yes. Thank you." Decker stepped out of the car, pulled up the app and paid the driver, leaving a hefty tip.

He took one look at the pub next to the posh location. *That* was his ideal first date location. A relaxed pub. A few beers and fish and chips.

But he'd hired the matchmaking firm to find him a perfect match. A way to skip the rotation of first dates at pubs. Andilet was the best in the business for a reason.

Or so they claimed.

He stepped into the restaurant, greeting the older gentleman at the podium.

"Your date is already here." The man offered a smile but there was a hint of judgment.

Am I that late?

Decker looked at his wristwatch. Ten minutes late to a first date; not the best start.

He rounded the corner and stopped as the beauty he'd bumped into this morning raised her dark brown gaze to greet him. She was still dressed in yellow. The large yellow flower in her hair still perfectly placed.

The gold eye shadow she had on was new. This morning it had been a cool brown. A natural shade, maybe more work-appropriate. The gold made her deep chocolate gaze pop. He'd kept a goddess waiting. After spilling coffee on her toes.

Decker looked at her feet and heard her laugh.

"I tossed the shoes in the bin when I got back to my flat after work." The woman wiggled the low black heels. "I feel they looked far better than they felt. Even before coffee covered them."

His cheeks heated. "I am really sorry." He'd been late for a meeting, and he'd just gotten four emails from agents looking for pieces for their actresses. The awards season was months away, but that didn't mean people weren't already plotting to secure the best.

His assistant had gotten fed up with telling them they needed to wait for nomination announcements at least and passed them over to Decker. Frustration had coated him, and he'd barreled out of the car without looking.

"It's fine." She held out a hand, "Nice to meet you properly. I'm Fran…cesca."

"Francesca." The name sounded odd on her lips. "Is that what you always go by?"

Her cheeks darkened as she looked at their still joined hands. "I'm trying it out. Apparently its more elevated than Frankie." She pulled her hand back.

"Frankie." He took the chair opposite her. "I like

it. It suits you. Who told you not to use it?" His father had held unique ideas about status. His mother had made sure none of those thoughts lodged in Decker's psyche.

"Honestly," Frankie bit her lip, "Amelia suggested I transition to my given name."

Decker laughed. "Amelia wanted you to change your name. Oh, please. That is wild. I know they are the top matchmakers in the city, but that is a bit much."

Frankie let out a giggle. "Yes, but that is what everyone pays for." She gestured to the quiet tables around them. "Elevation."

"I was actually thinking as I walked in here that I'd prefer to be at the pub next door."

"Let's do that." Frankie grabbed her purse. "We've not ordered. We can leave a nice tip for the staff, so they don't feel slighted, and go have a beer and a chat."

"And maybe some fish and chips." Decker stood, dropping some money on the table. It wasn't strictly necessary, but the restaurant had booked them for a table that wouldn't be getting used.

"Fish and chips." Frankie made a face as she held a hand over her heart. "I would not have thought the owner of Heughs Jewelry would want fish and chips."

"Why?" Decker held out his arm. Frankie hesitated for only a moment before slipping her arm through his.

She didn't say anything for a moment, then finally offered, "I guess I figured you had an *elevated* palate."

"Is fish and chips not an English staple?"

"That is certainly what tourists think. Though I will admit that fried fish and chips are better here than anywhere else I've been." Frankie slipped out of his arm as he opened the door of the pub.

"Where have you been?" Decker hadn't had the opportunity to travel as much as he'd like. His mother and stepfather had made their way across Europe and North America while his mother was still able. They'd planned to travel Asia this year but her health was slipping.

And Decker, well, Decker traveled for work and nothing else.

"All over. My parents are academics. My dad actually has several bestselling books on economics." Frankie let out a small shudder.

"Economics not your thing?" He honestly didn't care much for the subject, either. Decker had taken courses at university. One did not take over major corporations without knowledge of the markets, but that did not mean he enjoyed the subject.

"It's very dry." Frankie sighed as she slid up to the bar.

That was an incredibly diplomatic response.

"I'd like a Peroni and some fish and chips."

The bartender took Frankie's money, then looked at Decker.

"Make it two." He took the beers, passing one to Frankie, and they moved to the back of the pub to find a table.

Frankie climbed into the high bar chair and looked at the beer in front of her. "Think Amelia will be cross that we ditched the restaurant?"

"I don't really care about what Amelia thinks. We're the ones looking for a partner, right?"

"Right." Frankie took a sip of the beer, then another deeper one.

Nerves could do funny things on first dates but there was something about the action that worried him.

Come on, man. It's a first date. Don't look for more than it is.

"So, pub food?" Frankie smiled and leaned toward him.

Damn. This woman was a deity. And in the yellow, she glowed under the dim pub lights.

Decker leaned closer, too. "Want to know a secret?"

"Absolutely."

He gestured to the pub. "I spent most of my time at uni in places like this."

Frankie raised a brow. "Is that supposed to be the secret? You ate and drank in pubs at uni?" She laughed, a deep rich chuckle that ignited a cool place deep in his soul.

"I mean, I know it doesn't sound like much."

"It doesn't sound like anything." Frankie put her hand over his, then blushed and pulled back.

"I don't mind if your hand is on mine, or vice versa." Decker laid his hand on hers, grinning at the smile on her face as she met his gaze. This was a first date moment none of the others had had.

The other women had been nice. Stunning. Educated. But there hadn't been an instant feeling of anything. And he certainly would never have expected them to take him seriously when he talked about the pub.

"Did you spend your uni time in pubs like this?" Decker leaned just a hair closer only to feel his spirits drop when she pulled her hand away and picked up her beer.

"No. I didn't… Umm…" She looked toward the door and bit her lip. "My secret is that I didn't go to uni."

Many people didn't go to university, though he had to admit he'd never dated anyone who hadn't.

"What did you do instead?" It wasn't like she was confessing some great sin. Though the look on her face made him think she'd been told differently many times.

"A little of everything. I love drawing and creative outlets best but…" She looked away for a second. "My parents and sister are more than a little annoyed that I can't seem to make things stick. They call me Flyaway Frankie." She cleared her throat.

"A little of everything, huh." He'd done one thing and one thing only. His father lost Heughs Jewelry just before Decker turned thirteen. The man had become a walking shell of himself. And Decker had sworn he'd get the company back.

He'd gone to university, studied business and design. Earning first-class honors in both. Then he'd apprenticed at another firm, worked his way up fast—after all he'd grown up in, at the time, one of the most prestigious jewelry firms in the world.

No vacations. No personal life. Nothing until he'd captured his prize. Which he'd done four years ago with the help of a loan from a client. Last year he'd bought a rival company and paid off the loan. Now, he was on top of the world but had nothing else.

"Yeah. I was an actress for a while. Though my best role was body number two on a crime drama." Frankie giggled. "I laid on the floor for eight hours, six of which my body was covered with a sheet. Not using a mannequin felt a little like torture."

He laughed. "That does sound like torture."

"Yep. I was also a hand model." She held up her fingers, painted yellow.

"They are very attractive fingers."

Frankie rolled her eyes as she flexed them. But it wasn't a lie. He could absolutely see a print campaign for engagement rings with her hands in the center.

"I understand that is a lucrative field."

"It is." Frankie looked at her hands. "It is also nerve-racking. I use my hands every day. I had a panic attack once cutting leeks for a soup. The knife nearly sliced my thumb. Nearly! A nick would have ended my shoots for at least a month. Just because I was making soup."

He'd never considered that aspect of modeling. It made sense, in a weird way. "So you walked away."

"Yes." She tapped her long fingers on the table. "I've worked in just about every food service type in the country. Worked as a personal shopper, assistant. You learn a lot about—" she stopped herself from saying whatever was coming first and finished with "—people."

"And what do you do now?" This was fascinating. The woman had more experience than he did in many ways. She'd tried things. He'd won at one thing.

"I'm trying something new. Too soon to tell if it will stick." Frankie leaned toward him. "I've chatted all this time, what about you? What do you do besides jewelry?"

"Nothing." He held up a hand. He'd had this conversation so many times. Disappointed everyone. "I'm afraid I am terribly boring. I work. That is all."

"How dreadful." Frankie shook her head. "Well, then the next date we go on cannot be a pub or a restaurant. We must find you some sort of hobby. That way you won't be so dreadfully boring."

"Next date?" Decker raised a brow.

Frankie's cheeks darkened. "Assuming you want another date."

"I most certainly do." Before he could add on to that, the waitress brought over the fish and chips.

"This looks delicious." Frankie grabbed a chip and dipped it in the small pot of curry sauce she'd ordered with it. "Yes. Delicious."

His gaze was focused on her lips, the tiny piece of salt clinging to her full bottom lip. "Delicious, indeed."

CHAPTER TWO

YESTERDAY FRANKIE WOULDN'T have thought it possible to be more nervous for day two of a new job. Her stomach was flipping and the coffee she'd gotten just after getting on the tube tasted off. It wasn't the barista's fault. Whenever Frankie was nervous, food simply didn't have the same taste.

Her mother always said it was in her head. Frankie agreed, but that didn't make it less accurate.

The fish and chips last night—those were delicious.

Because Decker was so fun. And I was deceiving him.

Her brain warred with itself as she stepped up to the heavy door of Andilet. The door buzzed open before she could press the button.

"Amelia wants to see you."

Of course she does.

"Thanks, Patrice."

"Um… Francesca." The receptionist leaned forward.

Francesca. That was really who she was going

to be in the office. Francesca's feet wanted to bolt but Frankie forced herself to take a step toward the desk. "Yes?"

"Amelia isn't usually so uptight. In fact I enjoyed working for her until a few months ago, even though she calls me *Patrice* instead of Patricia."

So Frankie wasn't the only one with an "upgraded" moniker. Amelia might refuse to refer to her by Patricia but Frankie was doing it anytime their boss wasn't around.

Patricia's top teeth bit into her bottom lips as she glanced over her shoulder and then back at Francesca. "Are you all right? I know she sent you out with a client last night."

So Amelia didn't usually send newbies out as fake dates for high-profile clients. Frankie had suspected as much, but it was nice to confirm this was a one-off. Maybe the work environment would improve soon.

"Thanks for checking. I'm all right. We had fish and chips and beer." If it had been a real first date, she'd be checking her phone for a text to schedule the next one. But it wasn't real. And eventually, Decker was going to find that out.

"Fish and chips and beer, but Amelia always sets up dates at—"

"Patrice, we do not have time for gossip sessions. I told you to send Francesca to my office directly." Amelia's hands were folded and daggers shot from her icy blue eyes.

At least there wasn't coffee sloshing in Francesca's stomach as it rolled. "Sorry, I was just heading in to see you."

"Clearly not." Amelia turned on her heel, marching into her office.

Sorry, Patricia mouthed to Frankie but the damage was done.

Day two…off to a "great" start. Now would be a good time for the seemingly mythical Amelia that was good to work with to reappear.

If only.

"I need to know everything." Amelia was already sitting at her computer, hands on the keyboard.

If there were any humor available, Frankie might ask if this was an intelligence debriefing. One of her former roommates had enjoyed spy shows and the debriefings the agents went through were always so formal, tinged with tension as the spies inevitably were trying to hide something.

But there was nothing for Frankie to hide.

"It was a first date." Frankie slid into the same uncomfortable high-backed chair she'd sat in yesterday. "We had fish and chips and a few beers."

"Fish and chips?" The clicks of the keyboard stopped and Amelia's gaze bore into her. "Ten Tables does not sell fish and chips. Its upscale menu is available to exactly ten couples every night."

The rotating menu at Ten Tables was the talk of London when it had opened two years ago. The society pages had raved at the idea. Frankie's roommate at the time, a flight attendant for British Airways, had called it ridiculous. She said the place wouldn't last five years.

She served first-class passengers on international flights that sometimes paid more than twenty thousand pounds for their seats. Her claim was that they liked unique but unique wears off. And since the "common" folk couldn't afford it, even if they wanted pretentious dishes, it was a dead man walking on opening day.

"Yes, I know. But Decker wanted fish and chips and the pub next door—"

Amelia was out of her seat, palms flat on the desk. "You took Decker Heughs, of Heughs Jewelry, to a fish-and-chips pub."

People went for fish and chips all the time. Hell, there were places that made their annual living on tourists coming to find the "authentic" British comfort food.

"Technically, Decker took me." It had been his idea. Yes, she'd jumped at it. Yes, the night had slipped into a comfortable rhythm. Yes, she'd had to remind herself it wasn't real anytime he leaned toward her.

And this morning, she could still describe the spicy scent that wafted off him. Cinnamon and ginger. It had curled her toes as his full lips got closer to hers. She'd forced herself to pull back over and over again when her fingers wanted to lock with his.

"Decker Heughs took you to a pub?"

"Why is that so hard to believe? The Old Dog is right next door. The smell of fried—"

"The Old Dog!" Amelia growled as she slammed back into her chair. "Our longest running client…" She pulled a hand over her face.

"Perhaps he is the longest running client because he wants to do things like this? I mean, there isn't much in his file." Frankie didn't want to upset her boss but seriously, this wasn't a big deal.

"You were supposed to get information to fill that file."

"And I did." Frankie kept her tone level when all she wanted to do was slap the desk and tell Amelia to find someone else for this escapade.

And she might have, if her sister hadn't gotten promoted yesterday and a former roommate hadn't texted the great news that she was expecting her first child. Frankie hated that her initial reaction to both had been frustration. To see them as reminders that she seemed behind life's curve.

So she bit back everything she wanted to unleash on her boss. "He ate every bite of fish and chips. Drank a beer and chatted."

"About?"

"Nothing really." Frankie shook her head. "The reason there are no hobbies listed, no favorite foods, no personality in his file is because he has focused only on the jewelry business. I told him date two is finding a hobby for him."

"A hobby." Amelia tapped her fingernails on her desk. "What kind of hobby would be right for Decker Heughs?"

"I kinda thought I might run a few past him, see what sounded good to him." As soon as the words were out, Frankie knew they were the wrong ones.

"When they pay for Andilet's services, they expect us to handle everything."

And for the price, we should.

But hobbies were unique. Personalized. At least the ones that people liked long term.

Frankie's wrist buzzed and she looked at the text on her smartwatch. She felt the smile spread as she read the note from Decker.

"No personal messages during work." Amelia's sigh coated the office.

"Technically this is work. Decker is asking when we can see each other again."

"You gave him your number? Frankie, it was not a real date."

She didn't need to be reminded of that. But it was real for Decker. And that made her heart slump a little more. The man didn't deserve Andilet lying to him, even if it was to find the perfect partner for him.

Perfect partner...an elusive woman he'd hired the agency to find. Her chest tightened and the air in the room heated.

No, I am not jealous after one fake date.

"He asked for it. What was I supposed to say?

No would have indicated the date didn't go well. *Yes* and suddenly I'm the one in trouble here." Frankie crossed her arms. She'd had enough. Less than two days on the job and her boss was an absolute nightmare.

"I did not ask for this. In fact, you hired *me* for a very different position. Something I have in writing and I am willing to go to the Trading Council over. I am certain an employment tribunal inquiry would go in my favor."

Amelia's face fell and her angry demeanor collapsed. She closed her eyes and took a deep breath.

I am going to get fired.

Two days would be a new record. The shortest position Frankie had held to date was as a home health aide. That was a week. Hadn't even made it past the orientation. She couldn't handle blood or body fluids. Catalina had laughed so hard.

"You're right." Amelia opened her eyes. "I am not usually this overbearing. I swear it. I just… I just can't clear him. I am failing. My family has run Andilet for four generations. We are the top but people aren't reaching out like they used to. Dating apps. The twenty-first century…it's all digging into our bottom line."

Frankie didn't know what to say. The world was changing and you had to change with it. Luckily, Amelia didn't seem to need an answer.

"Decker Heughs has sunk so much money into this and nothing." She gestured to the computer.

"I have a one hundred percent success rate. A hundred percent. *If* you don't count Decker Heughs."

"If you look at our books, he's paid an outrageous sum and if he asks for it back… Which he is within his right to do as there is a clause in the contract allowing a refund if he doesn't have a partner in the first year. And we are *well* past that. If he calls in the amount…" Amelia sucked in a breath and Frankie could practically hear the woman's heart beating from across the desk.

Perfection was a rough drug. Catalina had an addiction to it, too. Perfection when your company might be on the line was a recipe for disaster.

"Focus on what we know about him and accept what has worked with others isn't working for Decker." It seemed like such an easy statement. However, Frankie had seen Catalina lose her mind the night before a med board announcement. So certain that everything she'd worked for was about to crash and burn. Amelia was clearly cut from the same cloth.

Her boss let out a breath and pointed to her watch. "What does the text say?"

"Had a great time. When are we finding me a hobby?" Frankie smiled as she relayed the message.

Not a real date, Frankie.

"Hobby. All right, after spending the evening with him, what do you recommend?" Amelia turned to the computer, ready to type whatever Frankie came up with.

"Honestly, no idea. The man has designed jewelry and worked to take back his father's company since he was a teen."

Frankie herself enjoyed crochet. She had a whole army of little stuffed creatures on her windowsill. Catalina thought it was silly. Maybe it was, but it brought a smile to her face every time she completed a furry friend and put it with the others.

Decker didn't strike her as a yarn enthusiast.

"We could arrange a date at the art museum—or a touristy idea to see the crown jewels."

Neither of those felt right. Particularly the last one. The man spent all day with gems, the point of a hobby was something completely different.

"What about geocaching?" One of Frankie's classmates at secondary school had gotten really into it. Somehow, she could see the man who'd downed his fish and chips in the back of an ancient pub hunting for items strangers placed around the city.

"Geocaching? You mean the thing where you use a GPS receiver?"

"Yep. It's outdoors. Unique. I know for a fact the man has never done anything like it and bonus—" Frankie held up her phone "—we already have built in GPS receivers. I download an app and off we go! Should I text him back?"

"Yes, but tell him that the agency will set up the date. You've already reached out with an idea." Amelia held up a hand before Frankie could argue.

"I know you exchanged numbers but this is a matchmaking service and the rules are the first three dates are through us. Plus, this isn't real."

"Right. Good plan." Frankie hoped the disappointment radiating through her wasn't obvious. So she had a crush on the man she'd eaten fish and chips with. A crush was passing. It was nothing.

Nothing.

Geocaching. Decker had searched multiple websites trying to find out what the date Frankie had planned for him even meant. He'd thought she was joking about the hobby.

And even if she wasn't, he hadn't figured she'd pick something like this. When Decker thought of hobbies, he thought crafts. Such a limited thought, but his mother knitted any free moment. His old room had been transformed into her yarn supply closet when he got his own place.

It was a hobby that was shifting now. Some days she could go on as though nothing was different… others she forgot the basic stitches and counts she'd done since childhood.

The bad days were few and far between right now. But soon… Decker needed her to see him happy in love. Needed her to know it was going to be okay.

"Ready?" Frankie stepped next to him on the ledge by the tube where they'd agreed to meet. Today's outfit was white linen pants and a lavender crop top that hugged her chest far too perfectly.

Her natural hair was wrapped in a yellow hair wrap with the curls showing up top. She was gorgeous. Perfection.

"I feel a little underdressed." He looked down at his jeans, knowing that compared to the beauty beside him, he looked less than dapper.

"You look wonderful." She started to reach for his hand, then pulled back.

He looked at her long fingers but didn't reach for her, either. This was new. Exciting but new. He didn't want to overstep.

"I worked for a designer and now I see clothes as a statement. I can't stop myself. My sister calls it pretentious." She pointed toward the park where they were hunting the cache.

"Why is enjoying your clothing choice pretentious? Is it a sibling thing?" Decker had grown up an only child shuttled between his two homes. The few friends he'd had growing up were also only children.

They'd bonded at the expensive boarding school his father had insisted on. And disappeared the moment his family's status did.

A few reached out now and then. Looking for jewelry or a business connection. It was rough to realize most people only wanted you for what you could give them.

"Those are two very separate questions." Frankie's soft giggle made him laugh, too.

"I suppose they are. But I would like an answer." Now he did reach for her hand. For a moment he thought she'd pull back but she didn't. "As long as you're okay with it."

"Liking your clothes is not pretentious, unless you expect others to comment or do the same. I've known people who took great care selecting outfits. Hell, the papers constantly critique the royal family and celebrities on their outfits. And more than one person makes a living decoding the hidden messages that might or might not be there." Her words flowed in one seemingly long breath. Her passion clear.

Frankie took a big breath and then started again, "On the other hand, I've known men and women who throw on whatever is first in their closet for the day and that is it. Nothing wrong with that approach, either. It is really about what makes you happy."

Without thinking, he broke the connection with their hands and wrapped his arm around her shoulder. "And how does that work with your sister?"

Frankie leaned her head against his shoulder as they walked into the park. No words, just her head on his shoulder. Her stance was tight. Not second-date tight, but family-expectations tight.

Decker understood that invisible weight. He'd

lived with it every day when working to earn back his father's company. He hated feeling it in Frankie.

"My sister is a doctor." Frankie slipped from his arms and pulled out her phone. "A pediatric surgeon to be more accurate."

The accuracy mattered to her sister and had been pointed out several times, if he had to make a bet.

"Catalina is the first born. The one named after my mother's passion, Catherine of Aragon. Mom is considered the greatest modern historian on the first wife of King Henry VIII. Catalina lives up to all their expectations." Frankie pointed to her clothes. "And I dress fancy."

She bit her lip before giggling. It wasn't a fun laugh, though. It was a cover. A flimsy bandage over a deep emotional wound. "I mean designing clothing is fun and all, but Catalina saves lives. Literally. She wins."

"Why is it a competition?" Decker tilted his head, examining the darker color along Frankie's cheeks.

Now the laugh was genuine. "That is the most only-child statement I've ever heard." She opened the app she'd texted him to get. "We are geocaching not going over childhood trauma."

"Fair." He grabbed his phone from his back pocket, opened the app and stared at the GPS coordinates she'd sent him to load. "I have no idea what I am doing here, Frankie." The light blinked a little faster when he pointed it one way and then the other.

"You've never done this before. Of course you don't know what you are doing." She held up her phone, and after a quick explanation, she put it back in her pocket. "Where are we going?"

"Umm." Decker stared at the blinking light. Where were they going?

He took a step to the right and the light shifted, indicating they were headed in the wrong direction. "Not that way."

"Not that way," Frankie echoed. She leaned over his shoulder, looking at the app. Her cinnamon scent poured straight into his soul.

"It's hard to concentrate when you are touching me."

She jumped back. The exact opposite of what he wanted.

"That wasn't a complaint, honey." He winked and wrapped an arm around her waist.

Frankie stiffened in his embrace and he dropped his arm immediately.

"Sorry." Frankie swallowed. "I like when you touch me. I do. I…" She looked behind her, worried someone might catch them.

"It's only our second date, Frankie. You can be nervous about the whole thing still. No hard feelings."

"No hard feelings, really?" She tilted her head, "Or are you saying it's fine now, but I'll get a text telling me off later or be ghosted—" She stopped and ran a hand over her mouth.

Decker got the distinct impression she wanted to clasp her fingers over her lips and was barely restraining the urge.

"Sorry."

"That is far too many sorries, Frankie." Decker hated the implications of her rant. His college sweetheart had once complained that while Decker got to walk around in the world without a thought, she went around calculating her safety in every activity. "You have a boundary. Nothing wrong with that."

"You seem so perfect. How are you still single?"

Now it was his turn to laugh. "That is the question I keep asking Amelia. Or rather the one she asks me. I have no idea. Maybe I was just waiting for the right person to walk into Andilet."

Frankie bit her lip and looked away. "Maybe."

She took a breath, but when she looked back at him, there was a hint of something in her gaze. A longing? A hurt? A something.

Stop looking for things that aren't there, Decker!

They'd touched on far deeper discussion points than he'd ever hovered near with other dating companions.

He looked back at the app. "I think we are supposed to go over to the fountain." He held it out, far too pleased when Frankie stepped right next to him.

Her body was so close. A trust. One Decker had no intention of breaking.

"It's blinking hard for a second, then stopping and starting again."

"That means we've arrived." Frankie pointed to the sign in front of him. It was a basic sign. A brief history of the fountain. One that, like many things in London, was old. A modern and historic city all at once.

He read the sign. "It was erected after a battle. Humans always seem to erect monuments to tragedy after the fact, instead of trying to avoid it."

"We are a fickle species, for sure." Frankie hit his hip with hers.

The connection was brief but burned. He wanted to hold her. Kiss her? Would she taste as sweet as she looked?

"However, we aren't here for the historical information. We are here for the cache." She looked at the sign. "It has to be here somewhere."

"Be here?"

"Yes. A lot of times, the person who creates the cache hides it. That's part of the fun. You know where it's at, but still have to search."

"Okay. Like a puzzle." Decker bent on the other side of the sign. The back was stone, weatherworn. Just like the front but without the writing on it. Decker ran his hand along the ground behind the stone and a silver chain caught his eye.

"Frankie? Maybe I found something." Decker

pulled on the chain. It wasn't taut but it was attached to something.

A small can, no larger than a sardine tin, popped out of the leaves.

"You found it!" Frankie clapped as she looked at the can.

"What now?" The app had no place to mark it. Nothing other than the small blinking light that kept its motion up.

"You open it." Frankie shook her head.

That was fair. And rather obvious—once she stated it.

"Clearly." He stuck his tongue out, enjoying the grin she gave him. A tiny notebook and golf pencil were tucked inside along with a congrats note.

"It says that we sign our names and add the date." He put his name and Frankie's, the date, a little heart. The heart was an extra. An in-the-moment thing.

Something he'd never done. Schoolgirls with crushes did such things.

Well, I do have a crush on her. A big one.

Her gaze caught the heart and he watched her cheeks darken just a hair. "Do you want to try the next one on our map?"

"Yep." He was certain geocaching wasn't the hobby for him, but spending the day with Frankie absolutely was. "Lead on."

CHAPTER THREE

DATE NUMBER THREE. Third date. The final date.

At least, this was where all of Decker's other dates had ended. He'd never been overly concerned by it. That definitely said something.

He had a track record. He knew that. He'd begun to expect each woman to alert the office that he was not their match after the third date. The spark that might be there had obviously been gone by the end of each one. Or maybe his expectation of rejection killed it?

Perhaps he was a self-fulfilling prophecy. He expected the third date to go poorly and therefore it did. But not tonight. Tonight the streak broke.

At the bar.

Frankie's text hit his phone, and Decker's stomach rolled. This third date mattered. Something was different about Frankie. He wasn't sure what but there was no way he was screwing this up.

On my way. See you in five.

He hit Send but just before he put his phone away another text popped in.

Pierce family ticked on order. They say it was due today not next week. Our books show next week.

His assistant Miranda's text was short and to the point. It wasn't really the Pierce family. Leona, the matriarch, was the one calling the shots. No doubt she'd railed at Miranda for at least thirty minutes. If the Pierce family, or really Leona, hadn't given Decker a loan, Heughs Jewelry wouldn't be. Plus they dropped obscene amounts of money on pieces every few months. Still there were days when Decker dreamed of telling them off—not that it would ever happen.

If our books show next week, then it is next week. Look through my email files. I have a folder for the family. Find the contract and my emails and forward them along. Overtime plus ten pounds an hour for going in, tonight.

Normally he'd head over to placate them, but he couldn't miss the date with Frankie. He was already late.

He hurried past the front door and found her, already with a drink, sitting at a back table.

"Sorry, my assistant texted. Problem at the office."

"Do you need to leave?" Frankie's gaze fell to the pint. Not starting date three off on a win.

"No. Plus. I have plans." He'd called the match-making office and had Andilet set this up. He was looking forward to date number four when they could handle the details themselves.

"Plans?" Frankie raised a brow. "What kind of plans?"

"The secret kind. At least for the next—" he looked at his watch, then smiled at her "—ten minutes."

She opened her mouth but whatever she was about to say was interrupted by the bartender's yell. "If you are here for the ghost hunt, cash out your tab now and head to the back lobby."

"A ghost hunt. Tell me the ten-minute surprise is actually a ghost hunt."

"Well, it wasn't ten minutes, but yes." He looked at her drink. "Is that on a tab?"

"No. Just the one. So, patio?" She grabbed the pint and his hand. "I've never been on a ghost hunt. Is this a walking tour or do we get EMF readers and all the gear?"

Decker squeezed her hand, so happy with the press of her palm in his. He'd booked this on a whim. Something he'd never done. It seemed important that the date be unique.

Amelia had pushed back on the idea. Claiming Andilet had never done such a thing. Decker had offered to handle it himself. That had gotten her moving.

"I have no idea. I googled best ghost hunts and this one was top of the list. If I'd known you'd be so into it, I'd have researched harder. I was just looking for something unique and had Amelia set it up."

Frankie pursed her lips.

"You want to do something else?" They'd disappointed the matchmaking firm with their first date. Amelia had been professional when reminding him that contractually Andilet was required to handle the first three.

"No. I want to stay. Hell, yeah. I mean, it's not exactly something I tell people on the first or second date but ghouls, ghosts, the great beyond, fascinating." She was practically bouncing as they walked onto the porch. "My mom was always frustrated because I wanted to do the ghost walks at historical sites. Said it was historical tourist nonsense. You get more out of libraries and ancient texts, Francesca."

The tone on the last line was a clear mimic.

He dropped her hand and wrapped his arm around her shoulders. "I suspect for historians that is accurate, but this is supposed to be fun."

Frankie leaned her head on his shoulder as they joined the small group at the back of the pub. "I don't know that it is accurate, though." Her head popped back up and there was a sad look to her eyes.

He squeezed her tighter. "Don't keep it in. Why do you not think it's accurate?"

And put your head back where it was. He barely managed to catch that plea.

Frankie looked over her shoulder, like her mother might step out with a lecture before she squared her shoulders. "Most of these hunts are local history. The things that don't make the textbooks. Snippets from locals. My mother can, and has, given hours-long lectures on King Henry the VIII and Cathrine of Aragon's marriage. Their divorce. The number of stillborn children she lost, her refusal to call herself anything other than the Queen of England and Henry's lawful wife until the day she died."

"They are one of history's most interesting couples." Decker had paid attention in school but he knew only the basics, and the salacious bits about the wives Henry sent to the scaffold. That stuff stuck out to adolescent boys.

"Pish." Frankie waved a hand like she was pushing away the logic he'd used. "They are *well-documented*. That does not mean they were the most interesting. What about the baker's wife who clubbed him over the head when she found him in the back with the poor maid?"

"That is not a story I know. Where did that happen?"

"All over." Frankie let out a sigh. "I mean, I don't know any specifics on a baker's wife, but men have been cheating on their spouses and loved ones since time began. There was an Italian woman that was finally sentenced to death after she helped more than three hundred women poison their husbands. Where are the three hundred stories of what drove those wives to the poisoner?"

"What a lovely thought on our third date?" He didn't manage to keep a straight face as Frankie laid her hand over her mouth.

"Oh." Her cheeks darkened and she looked around, more than one couple seemed to be enjoying the interlude. "I guess it wasn't overly romantic. Good thing I don't know any poisoners."

There was no way he could control the laugh bursting from his throat. Third date. Ghost hunt and Frankie alluding to the fact that she wasn't a threat *only* because she didn't know any poisoners.

"Want to end the date now?" Frankie let out a sigh. "Or can we at least go on the ghost hunt before you *ghost* me?"

His arms wrapped around her waist and, when she didn't hesitate, his soul took flight. The entire audience vanished as her body pressed against his. "That was both the most terrifying and sexiest exchange I've ever had. If you think I'm ghosting you after that, Frankie…" His lips brushed her forehead.

"We are heading down to the basement now." The director of the tour's voice was a little raised. To catch everyone's attention…probably.

But it felt like he was breaking up the moment between them. *Not cool.*

"You will each be given a pair of flashlights, an EMF reader and a ghost box. There are four tunnels you can choose to investigate. Each is about half a kilometer long and none of them branch out, so you cannot get lost. In the late medieval era, a jail resided here and while records are sparse—"

Frankie's hip struck Decker's, reinforcing her point about people vanishing from the records.

"If the EMF goes off, you can use the ghost box to see if there is a ghost around. Heads up, the readers will detect your gadgets, so go ahead and turn them off now."

Turn them off.

The office was always able to reach Decker. He wasn't sure when his cell had last been in airplane mode, let alone off.

"Decker?" Frankie had already taken her phone out of the jeans hugging her hips in all the right places, pressed a button and slid it back in her pocket. "Everything all right?"

"My phone is never off." Just looking at the power button was making his finger twitch. When had he last been unreachable? And Miranda was figuring out the mess at the office.

What if she needed him?

"Does your family need to reach you?" Such an innocent question.

One that made him wish that were the answer. His mother or stepfather needing him was a good excuse but that was all it was. The hunt lasted for two hours.

Miranda was handling the Pierce case. Getting their order aligned. She was more than capable. Besides, his books were right and Heughs Jewelry never missed a delivery.

"Do we need to just head back into the pub?" Frankie's voice was already resigned. The other couples and groups of friends had grabbed the equipment and headed on.

"No." He was not disappointing this woman. He pressed the button and slid his phone back in his pocket.

"I am not going to ask if that was hard." Frankie kissed his cheek, an impulsive move her eyes instantly showed she was rethinking.

So Decker bent, skimming his lips along her cheek. "I am so looking forward to this." He pulled her toward the one bag of supplies left.

A few hours where no one could reach him would let him focus solely on Frankie.

She'd kissed him. On the cheek, but still. This wasn't a date. Not a real one.

He thinks it is.

Pain shot through her lower lip and Frankie forced her teeth to let go of their death grip. Amelia had been very clear. She was to find out why Decker's dates always dipped out after the third date.

Not only was she doing a piss-poor job on that

assignment; she was enjoying herself far too much. Hell, if this were an actual third date, she'd already be plotting to end the night with a kiss. Or invite him up to her flat for a while.

"All the groups have picked a tunnel. No idea if they are all in one or spread out. Where should we go?" Decker's hand was bright in the flashlight as he pointed down the access points.

"Tunnels feels like a bit of an exaggeration." Frankie couldn't stop the shudder running down her spine as she stared at four cutouts in the wall no more than three feet wide and five or so feet tall. "You're going to have to duck."

She'd wanted to do this. Wanted to do it still— but there was something about seeing the tunnels. Knowing that hundreds of men and women had resided down here waiting whatever fate. The whole place felt off.

Decker's arm wrapped around her, chasing some of the chill away. It would be nice—if Frankie didn't enjoy it so much.

Not a date. Not a date.

There was nothing wrong with this man. He was respectful. Intelligent. Fun. Not hard on the eyes. *At all.*

"I can't believe people used to live down here." Decker swung the flashlight from left to right.

"*Live* is very relative. They were imprisoned here. Survived, or not—given that we are on a ghost hunt—is more accurate." Frankie's mother's focus was the courts. The wealthy class that could pay for better accommodations than what was around them. This was where the unfortunate everyday people landed.

"True." Decker's flashlight moved so its beam was pressed into hers. "Which tunnel?"

She shuddered—again. What was wrong with her? The idea of a ghost hunt was exciting. She'd practically bounced when he'd told her the plan. But now that they were down here, knowing this was an old prison, her body wanted to run back up the stairs rather than go into the tunnels.

"What if we investigate this room?" Decker turned on the EMF reader. "Everyone is in the tunnels, and there was activity out here, historically. Or we could go back upstairs, have a pint."

"No." Frankie looked at the EMF reader. "Let's stay in here. You're right. There were people living and interacting in this room. The tunnels, I don't know, I just…"

"No need for explanations. You don't want to go down them. That is fine. In fact it is all the answer you need to give." Decker handed her the EMF reader, and wrapped his free arm around her while his other hand held the flashlight.

How did every third date this man went on end with the woman telling Amelia he wasn't their match?

"So, do you think we ask if there are ghosts

here?" Decker pulled her a little closer. "Or do we wait for the EMF reader to do something?"

Frankie held the machine out in front of her. It bounced a little but didn't really do much. "Maybe? Never been on one of these. I saw an American reality show where two plumbers hunted ghosts as their side gig. But it was obviously pretty scripted."

"Right." Decker took a deep breath, then set up the small ghost box. "Ready?"

"Now you are the one that sounds unsure." Frankie leaned her head against his shoulder. For comfort. That was all.

Decker chuckled but the nerves were obvious in it. "You know, if you had asked me before we came down here if I believed in ghosts, I'd have told you I have no evidence for them."

"Really? I am an absolute believer. Too many stories throughout history. Whether it is a soul left behind or someone repeating a lived experience, trapped in a loop, no idea." Frankie had never discussed her belief in the other side. In fairness none of the guys she'd dated had asked.

And I'm nearly as bad as Decker on dating.

She'd made it past the third date several times. But Frankie had gotten serious exactly once. And come back to their shared flat to find him in bed with her former best friend. Lesson learned. No sticking around or getting close.

She was fine on her own. Mostly. Sometimes it

was lonely, but that was better than finding your boyfriend in bed with someone you thought you could trust.

Decker flipped on the ghost box.

"Home."

"Home."

"Home."

"Three times." Decker tilted his head looking at the now quiet box. "Think it's broken?"

"No." Frankie wrapped her arms around herself. This place was more spooky than anything. "If you were in here, wouldn't your only thoughts be of home."

The place was unsettling.

"Yeah. I guess. That and sun." He shuddered.

"At least I am not the only one who's spooked!" Frankie moved closer.

"It's spooky down here." He looked toward the tunnels. "Spookier in there I bet."

"Bet."

"Dead."

"Bad."

The words squawked from the box and she jumped. Decker's arms were around her in an instant. "Hey." His lips pressed to the top of her head. "You're okay."

"I liked this idea. I jumped at it." It felt silly to mind what was coming out of the box.

"Bad."

"Bad."

"Bad."

The word echoed from the box three times.

"I wouldn't mind heading back to the pub." He tightened his grip on her.

She wasn't sure he really meant that, but she was taking the offer.

"Sounds good."

They exited quickly.

The attendant looked at them as they passed the box back. "You stay in the main area?" She raised a brow, the tilt of her lips showing no surprise that they were handing the box over.

"Yeah." Frankie looked at the now very quiet box. "Why?"

"The only people who ever come up quickly are the ones in the main area. The tunnels, you get a few things. Hints of whatever is beyond the veil. In the main area, it always starts with *home*, then says things like *bad, evil, go, dead.*"

"We got *home, dead* and *bad.*" Decker cleared his throat and pulled her a little closer.

"Yeah. We don't know who is there, but they are not happy. We brought in a medium once, but she only said the spirit was evil and not willing to talk." The woman shrugged, "I thought she was full of it for the first year I ran the tour. But everyone who chooses not to venture into the tunnels comes up here well before their time is up."

"Guess we should have chosen a tunnel," Frankie muttered.

"But then you might not be in my arms right now." Decker pressed his lips to her temple.

Damn.

She liked standing in his arms. Liked staying with him. And she had to give him up.

The worst part was that she'd failed. She had no idea why he didn't pass muster with others. He was the perfect date.

No. The worst part was giving him up.

"Let's grab some pints and see if that drives the chill away." Decker grabbed her hand and pulled his phone free with the other.

He turned it on and immediately frowned.

"Everything okay? I can grab the beers. What do you want?"

Decker didn't look up from his phone. He was shaking his head. "No."

"What?"

"I have to go." He put the phone in his back pocket and walked out.

No goodbye. No look back. Nothing.

There it is.

"Think he has a wife at home?" The woman behind the counter was glaring after him.

"No." Frankie shook her head. "He said something before we started about a problem at the office."

"Don't let him sell you that." She waved a hand.

"That man went from *I am wrapping my arms around you* to *gotta go.* No goodbye."

As the recipient of the brush-off, Frankie hardly needed a recap.

CHAPTER FOUR

"HE JUST LEFT?" Amelia blinked, opened her mouth, closed it and just shook her head.

"Yep." Frankie still couldn't figure out how they'd gone from Decker holding her to nothing at all.

It stung. A fact she wasn't sharing with Amelia. This had been a job, and Frankie had succeeded. Heughs Jewelry was Decker's focus. It was his North Star.

And Frankie knew very few women who were willing to be second to a company—at least at the beginning. Maybe a few years after you met at the altar, but at the beginning most people wanted at least the illusion of primary importance.

"I imagine something similar occurred with the others. Maybe not as drastic. At least I hope not, but still." Frankie shrugged. "Need anything else from me?"

Not that I haven't already gone over and above for the company.

"No." Amelia's gaze was glued to the computer screen. "I don't know how we fix this."

Frankie stood. It wasn't a question. But she felt honor bound to add something. "*We* don't. Decker has to fix this. Until he realizes he needs to place a partner at least on an even playing field with his company, each date will be doomed."

"Not if we find a transactional partner who only wants to marry rich and never cares if they are with their partner."

"No!" The reaction was too much. Amelia's words were accurate. Horrid, but accurate. That didn't mean Frankie wanted such a union for Decker. He deserved more.

"You didn't catch feelings for him, did you?" Thankfully Amelia didn't look up from her screen when she asked.

Frankie straightened her shoulders, adjusting the purple skirt she'd picked out for today. When she answered, she wanted to make sure her voice didn't falter.

"I like him. He is a good person. Too focused on work, but he wasn't that way on our first two dates." Hell, even for most of the third date, he had been fantastic.

It was just the end. Like a wall had crashed between them.

"I've asked him to come in today," Amelia said. "Or rather, I sent a note to his assistant. She let me know he was in the office all night and she doubted he'd be in. But she will pass along the information."

"I don't want to be here for the meeting." The words were out and she could tell by Amelia's frown that she didn't appreciate the interruption.

"You will be here, Francesca. We will sit him down and explain what you learned. I do not like the deception—"

"The deception you forced on me." Frankie crossed her arms.

Why didn't I just leave when I stood up?

Now she was in an awkward position, feeling more like a child awaiting a scolding than a discussion with her supervisor.

"Yes, Francesca, I am aware that I forced the issue. I will make sure Decker understands that, if you like." Amelia clicked a few more keys before lowering her glasses and looking Frankie over.

"Yes, I would like him to know that." It likely wouldn't matter. When they told Decker, he'd probably hate Frankie. And she wouldn't blame him.

She hadn't meant to lead him on, but she wasn't lying to herself. She'd liked hanging out with him. Liked laughing with him. Liked when he held her.

"And are you prepared for him to ask for his money back?" If he called in the debt the company owed, Andilet might be done.

And I'll be back on the job hunt.

"He is not going to. I am going to explain everything. He will understand and we will set up his next date with more accuracy." The clipped words did not hide the shake in her hands.

She was terrified he'd call in the debt.

Frankie wasn't positive how knowing the company came first for Decker—and thus leave a date without even a goodbye—was going to magically make his perfect spouse appear, but that was a job for Amelia.

"Am I beginning my actual training today?" She could sit back down, but Amelia hadn't offered and Frankie wasn't inclined to stay any longer than she had to.

"Yes. I've got Emma ready to take you through things. When I hear from Decker's assistant, I will let you know. If he texts you first, set up a meeting here."

He hadn't texted Frankie this morning. No apology late in the evening when he realized he'd left her high and dry.

That's assuming he noticed.

He wasn't going to text.

Her stomach twisted and she barely controlled the tears that wanted to fall.

She hadn't been stood up by a real date. It was pretend. The fact that he didn't know that didn't change reality.

"I don't think he will reach out, but if he does, I'll be sure to let him know that you want to set up a meeting." Frankie turned on her heel before Amelia could offer a reply.

She was a matchmaker-in-training now, not a pawn in this game. Gripping the handle, she took a deep breath and pulled the door open. Today her career started *for real*.

"Frankie!" Decker's deep voice raced across the foyer.

She heard Amelia stand behind her, but Frankie didn't turn to look.

"Are you all right?" she asked. He was still in the same clothes he'd worn to the pub last night. There was more than a little stubble on his jawline and the bags under his eyes were deep purple. "Have you slept?"

"No. I got a delivery date on an order wrong. First time it's happened since I took over the company. I worked all night to get the piece crafted."

Amelia was pressing against her, but Frankie wasn't moving out of the way. In a moment, Decker was going to learn the matchmaking firm had so little faith in his ability to find a partner that they'd sent a new employee to scout him out.

He was exhausted. This conversation could, and should, wait until he was in a better headspace.

"You need to go home and get some rest. You can come back when you've slept."

"No." Decker took a few steps toward her as Amelia finally plowed her way past Frankie. "I assume you're here to tell them that I screwed up the third date. I know I did. I left with no warning and I just—" He ran a hand through his hair. "I just need you to give me another chance, Frankie."

"I'm afraid that's not possible, Mr. Heughs."

Amelia gestured for Decker to follow her into her office. "Francesca?"

"She prefers Frankie," Decker muttered as he walked past her.

Amelia looked at her, but didn't say anything as she slid back behind her desk. "Close the door, please."

Frankie looked at the door. If she closed it with her on the other side, would Amelia chase her down? Probably not. But she didn't want Decker alone with Amelia. In a few minutes he'd hate Frankie, but this conversation was not going to be an easy one.

She slid into the chair next to him, careful to keep her gaze on the corner of Amelia's desk.

"*Frankie.*"

She couldn't help but smile as he accentuated the nickname she preferred.

"I know I messed up. But—"

"They were not real dates." Amelia let out a sigh. "Mr. Heughs, Francesca is our newest matchmaker, and I asked her to go on three dates with you so we could determine what continued to go wrong with your matches."

There had to be a better way to say that, but honestly Frankie was at a loss for how to let it out any easier than that.

"What?" Decker reached for Frankie's hand. The brief connection was scalding.

Pulling back hurt even more. "I am so sorry."

Frankie looked at him, hoping her gaze might convey how much she meant the apology. "I am a matchmaker. Or I will be now that my job—"

"Isn't dating me?"

Her cheeks flooded with heat at his interruption. He got to respond to this however he wanted. "The day you spilled coffee on my feet—"

"What?"

Frankie ignored Amelia's interruption. "That was my first day. I wasn't expecting to…" She let those words die away. "I did enjoy our time together and I think you will make a wonderful partner, if you open yourself up to more than the jewelry business."

She held up a hand as she saw him shift, preparing for an interruption or just uncomfortable. "You have so much to offer." Frankie swallowed the lump in the back of her throat.

Offer to a partner that wouldn't be her. Why the hell was this so difficult?

"But you need to find you, too." She grabbed the tablet from Amelia's desk and pulled up his profile. "Hobbies? None. Food. Whatever."

"I didn't say whatever."

"You may as well have." Frankie set the tablet back down. Any minute now Amelia was going to interrupt this, probably even send her out of the room. If this was the last time she saw Decker, she wanted him to understand he had it in him to make somebody very happy.

"So the firm set me up with you to get intel." Decker tilted his head, his dark eyes boring into hers.

"Yes." Now it was Frankie shifting in her seat.

"Did you get enough?"

"What?" She must have misunderstood. Decker was leaning back in his chair now, relaxed. The angry explosion she was expecting wasn't materializing.

"Enough intel?" Decker crossed one leg over his knee and waved his hand. "Do you know why I'm always getting dumped on the third date?"

"You didn't get dumped."

"Because you weren't a real date, right?"

Heat coated her cheeks and Frankie looked at Amelia. Her boss shrugged. Frankie had taken control of a meeting that she'd specifically asked Amelia to handle.

"That was a low blow. I apologize." Decker crossed and uncrossed his legs. "I fear finding out I am such a failure, the firm needed a fake date to figure out why a difficult pill to swallow."

"That's understandable. You are kind. And funny, and gentle and an interesting date. Unless something happens with Heughs Jewelry which, given the company size and profile, will happen at least every few weeks." Frankie looked toward the door. When could she politely dismiss herself?

She wanted him to know his good qualities, but there was no way she wanted to listen to him plot how to find a partner with Amelia. That was a step too far on the bridge she was straddling.

"Careful, it sounds like you enjoyed our dates."

There was a look in his eyes that she couldn't quite decipher. This was the shrewd businessman. The one who'd reclaimed his father's prize in record time.

"I won't lie to you," she caught herself from leaning toward him, "I did."

"Great. Then that settles it." Decker slapped his hand on his knee. "Sounds like I need a dating coach. You up for the job?" He looked at Amelia, "I know you don't usually offer such services, but given my history, I think it's a good idea."

The buzz in her ears was deafening. There was no way she was hearing him correctly. No way she was listening to Amelia acknowledge what a good idea it was. No way this was happening.

"If this is a success, then offering another service to our customers…"

Amelia's words were lost in her brain's buzz as Frankie tried to process everything going on around her. How was she supposed to coach Decker? Make him into the perfect partner for a woman she never wanted to meet?

"Francesca, *Frankie*." Amelia cleared her throat as Decker shot her a glance. "Frankie will get the dates set up. She'll critique and offer you feedback at the end of each."

"That sounds perfect." Decker winked at Frankie.

It was absurd.

"I look forward to your texts, Frankie." Decker stood, looked like he might lean over to touch her, but pulled back and headed out the door.

"Well, that went fantastic." Amelia let out a breath as the door shut behind Decker.

"Fantastic? Fantastic? You signed me up to be his dating coach."

"Technically, *he* signed you up." Amelia leaned back in her chair. "I know you planned to be a matchmaker."

"That *is* the job you hired me for." Frankie bit her lip and fought to keep her breathing even.

"*But*," Amelia leaned forward on her desk, "if this goes well, you will be on the ground floor of the new department."

Ground floor. That was career-making. This was an open shot. *Her* shot.

"All right. But we are going on fun dates, nothing that borders on serious. This is coaching, not dating, not really." Whether she was saying that for Amelia or for herself, Frankie wasn't sure.

"Of course." Amelia turned back to her computer. Meeting adjourned, apparently.

Decker checked his phone as he stepped out of Andilet. He could breathe again.

He'd spent all night working on Leona Pierce's piece and adding a second piece as an apology. She'd been right. He wasn't sure what had caused him to mistype the delivery date. Little mistakes like that could cost a business—eventually.

As he was handing Miranda the necklace and earrings to wrap and deliver, she'd told him Andilet had been in touch to set up a meeting. It had jolted his memory. He'd looked at his phone to see nothing from Frankie.

He'd racked his brain trying to remember if he'd even said goodbye. The memory was blank.

Because I just ran off.

Decker had known Frankie was going to call it off. And for the first time, his heart had refused to let it happen. He'd marched to the meeting, with no plan but to plead for a second chance.

Frankie was dating him to get a read on him. That was fair. He was a businessman. One that could technically request a refund for services not delivered.

He had no plans to do that. After all, it wasn't Andilet's fault he was bad at this.

But he hadn't been so bad with Frankie. There was something there. Something between them. He was different with her.

I wasn't different on the third date.

If Decker were honest with himself, he understood where things had gone wrong on the other dates. His phone was always out. He'd responded to one or two emails—quickly—but still it was enough to show where his interest lay.

Not with Frankie, though. Not until last night.

Last night, he'd walked away without even telling the woman goodbye. That was rude in the extreme, but to do it to Frankie…

To the bright, laughing, gorgeous woman. It was inexcusable.

You free Saturday? Around six?

Absolutely, Frankie.

He'd come up with the dating coach thing on a whim. Frankie had liked their dates. And she'd started to lean toward him before catching herself. He wasn't willing to give her up. Not yet.

Meet me at this location. Wear something you don't mind getting dirty.

Wear something you don't mind getting dirty?
Decker shook his head as he typed back a text.

See you there.

He had no idea what Frankie had come up with, but he was looking forward to it.

He started to put his phone back in his pocket, just as a final buzz came through.

No looking at your work phone from six to nine on Saturday.

It was an easy enough request. So why was his stomach twisting at the simple words? Three hours. On a weekend. Decker gave a thumbs-up that he wasn't quite sure he felt.

Four days until he saw Frankie. Just four days.

The sun was on its descent as he walked across the bridge to the location she'd texted days ago. Funny how four days in theory was no time at all. A blip in a lifetime. Yet, when it was four days with no Frankie, no excuse to text, no sightings, no discussion, each twenty-four-hour period dragged.

"Frankie!" He held up a hand as she turned at the other end of the bridge.

She waved, then smiled and his chest eased.

For the first time in four days, he was able to fully exhale.

"Hi, Decker." She started to lean toward him, caught herself and offered her hand instead.

He gripped it, wildly aware of how unsatisfying it was not to pull her into his arms.

"You look beautiful."

"Thank you." Frankie nodded. "Complimenting your date is an excellent way to start conversations. But, most importantly, where is your phone, Decker?"

He tapped his back pocket. "In here and staying in here."

"Wonderful." She looked at her watch. "We need to head down to the café. The walk starts in twenty minutes." She passed him a pair of sturdy yellow gloves.

"Are we cleaning dishes at the café?" He looked at the gloves and chuckled. This was certainly an unusual date item.

Frankie's curls bobbed as she shook her head. "No. They are for mudlarking. Glass is very sharp and the Thames is not the cleanest."

"Wait, we are going mudlarking?" Surely this wasn't how they were spending their date?

"Yes."

"Like walking on the shore of the Thames, looking for old pottery and busted up artifacts?" He was counting on a romantic date. A way to subtly shift the relationship back to where it seemed to be going before he'd made such an ass of himself.

There wasn't a relationship.

No, he was not going to give into that desperate thought.

"Yes, you just described mudlarking, perfectly. Have you done it before?" Frankie beamed as they walked toward the café where a group was already standing outside.

"No. My mother and stepfather used to do it anytime they came to London. They have several clay pipes and broken dishes on their shelves." His stepfather loved the activity. His mother had gone along because she loved his stepfather. In the last few years, though, her gait was unsteady. Something they'd chalked up to age—until the memory problems started.

Frankie clapped her hands. "Clay pipes. How exciting. The most interesting thing I've found is some broken pottery that the university dated to the Victorian era. Nothing special, just some pieces the common folk used."

"I thought you said history was made up of the stories of the common folk? Something about the aristocracy seeming interesting only because we don't have records of the baker's wife whapping her husband over the head with a roller after she caught him tumbling the maid."

Frankie hit her hip against his. The connection was so brief, but the bulb of hope in his heart blazed. This idea might work.

"Remembering a date's interest." Frankie looked at her feet before focusing on the crowd gathering outside the café. "That is an excellent thing when getting to know someone. You really didn't need me to stay on as a dating coach. You know what you are supposed to do."

The tiny bulb of hope dimmed. She'd said she enjoyed their dates. He'd caught her leaning toward him.

But what if he'd misread the situation completely? Seen hints of more when she'd was just acting the part?

Am I the fool here?

"Frankie…"

"Over here, everyone!" the tour guide called out, but her focus was on him and Frankie. The two clear outliers.

She stepped up, her gaze rooted to the tour guide in front of them giving the safety lecture.

The words flew in Decker's ear and out the other. His mind, his gaze, everything focused on the woman beside him. She was rocking on her heels, the base of her neck was darker and she swallowed several times. He'd watched enough couples picking out engagement rings, wedding rings and sorry-I-messed-up rings to know she was nervous.

But was it I-want-to-bolt nervousness or the I-can't-believe-I'm-with-this-person-and-everything-is-going-right-and-what-if-it-fails kind?

His phone buzzed in his back pocket and his hand went to it. Before he could pull the offensive item out and turn it off, Frankie's hand was in his.

She wrapped her fingers around his, squeezed him but never looked in his direction.

No phones.

Frankie didn't say the words, but he heard them crystal clear through her raised-eyebrow gaze. He looked at their hands. Message received.

But she didn't drop her grip.

Not that he planned to complain.

CHAPTER FIVE

FRANKIE'S HAND STILL BURNED. Forty-eight hours later and her hand stung with the memory of his fingers wrapped through hers. His thumb moving ever so softly along the edge of her wrist.

Barely perceptible.

Maybe he wasn't even meaning to touch her like that. Maybe the soft sway of her heels as she tried to plant her ever-eager-to-flee feet created the magic touch.

She'd chosen mudlarking because it was the opposite of sexy. No dinner in a crowded pub where they might lean into each other. No ghost hunt where the spooks, or lack thereof, led to hugs and hands around waists.

No. They were sifting through trash. Literally!

And it was clear Decker hadn't enjoyed the activity, but he never complained. Never stopped searching the piles of garbage for some "treasure." He'd smiled when she held up a piece of broken pottery and made jokes throughout the day. Other men she'd dated would have marched off the second such an activity was even suggested. Decker made the best of it.

The man was nearly perfect. If he could find a way to place his business at least on level with his date, he'd be Andilet's most eligible bachelor tomorrow.

But if he can't break the habit for a while—

There was no use finishing that thought. They were from two different worlds. And she was his… dating coach? The term felt so awkward.

Only when I apply it to him.

The idea of a dating coach was mildly intriguing. She'd done so many things, worked so many jobs at all levels. Visited more than thirty countries, spoke four languages. Those skills could aid many people unsure of their place in this world.

She'd spent all day outlining the expansion. Adding dating coach to the company's services made sense. After all, Decker wasn't the only one stunted in the dating game. And given the deep pocketbooks of the individuals seeking Andilet's service, the added revenue was nearly limitless.

She flipped through the file she'd brought to the pub to go over. Technically she was off duty, but she was taking Amelia up on her offer. If this worked, then Frankie was on the ground floor of the new service.

I can make it mine.

It wasn't fashion design but this was a solid

enough choice. A safe-ish choice. A choice her family might approve of long term.

"What's so interesting in the file?" Decker's voice was warm on the back of her neck.

The smile crept across her face without warning as she turned to him. "What are you doing in this pub?"

He held up the pint and raised an eyebrow. "I would have thought it obvious? Pub. Beer."

Frankie looked around The Old Dog and raised her eyebrow to match his. "I can't imagine this is a place you frequent that often."

"It's where we went on our first not-a-real-date date." Color crept up Decker's neck and he cleared his throat. "You mentioned while we were there that you stopped by sometimes." He pointed to the file again. "That about me?"

"No." She knew everything there was to know from his file at Andilet. Hell, the most recent additions were typed from her notes. "Not everything is about you."

He threw his free hand over his heart, then took the seat next to her. "But I thought everything was." He winked as he moved his legs so they were on either side of her. The best way to sit and talk to a friend in a crowded bar.

Not the best way for me to avoid accidentally touching him.

"The dating coach service is mine. Or it will be when I find you—" her throat seized. Find you *a match*. Two extra words. Two little, stupid, easy words "—a match."

"So you are getting the dating service off the ground?" He leaned just a hair closer.

Why am I monitoring the millimeters?

At least he wasn't asking about the match she was supposed to be finding for him. "That is the plan; assuming this works?" She gestured between the two of them and looked at the bar. Her pint was empty. It was a built-in excuse. Tell Decker she was wrapping it up for the evening and head home to wallow.

Instead she caught the bartender's gaze. "Can I get another?"

The pint appeared a few seconds later.

"This?" He shifted a hair closer once again.

"Yes. This." She reached for the pint but didn't put any distance between them. "You are the longest running client."

"Yep. Heard that from Amelia enough. Don't need it from my—" he took a deep drag of the pint "—coach."

"Sorry." She'd said it more to remind herself of his status than anything else, but it wasn't exactly a moniker he was unaware of. "I've never had a career and this—" she tapped the file folder "—this has career all over it."

"Is it the career you want?"

She lifted her chin. Not really. This wasn't what

she'd imagined. But few people got exactly what they wanted. "Do you have the career you want?"

"I don't know." His words were soft. If they hadn't been so close, they'd have died in the pub's hustle.

Her mouth was open. Hanging wide open. She'd expected a brash response. Maybe even a whipping out of the phone she made sure stayed locked up when they were mudlarking. Not whatever answer that was.

"What does that mean?" The man had brought his father's jewelry empire back to life. Made it greater than before. Heughs Jewelry was his focus.

Decker tipped the pint up, sucking down the last dregs before putting it on the bar. Unlike her, he waved off the bartender as he walked toward them.

"I don't know. I mean, I like what I do. I am good at what I do. I achieved all my father's goals and then some, but was it my dream?" He shrugged, looked at the empty pint glass but didn't call the bartender over. "His dreams were my dreams or my dreams were his dreams. Sometimes I don't know where he ends and I begin."

Frankie put her hand on his knee. A comforting touch, but that didn't stop the lightning from shooting up her wrist. "You can do whatever you want, now."

"I know. And I still like the jewelry game. Boring meetings and all." He tapped a finger against her nose and started to lean toward her.

He's going to kiss me.

That wasn't supposed to happen but she was in too deep.

His lips moved past hers, hovering just by her ear. "Want to see a jewelry store? It's pretty magical after dark."

See the store? Her eyes clouded for just a moment. Damn. There wasn't a more ridiculous way to read the motion. She'd prepped for a kiss and he'd invited her to a jewelry store.

Just say no.

"Magical?" That wasn't no. "How can a store be magical?" She'd visited jewelry stores. Even gotten a private tour of the crown jewels with her mother. Not an overly enjoyable trip as her mother complained that none of the jewels from the Tudor era survived the execution of Charles the First in 1659.

"Yes." Decker stood and raised his hand. "Put her drinks on my tab and close it out."

"Oh, Decker, you don't—"

"I know I don't have to. But you're weighing how to tell me you don't want to go. The excuse of your tab staying open is gone."

Heat coated her cheeks. "Decker, I—"

"If you don't want to go, you don't have to. Just don't make up an excuse, okay?"

"I want to go." That was the problem. She wanted to have fun in a jewelry store with this man. Wanted to see what kept him so focused that he was unable to see through any date.

"Then…" He held out his hand.

She didn't hesitate, placing her hand in his and letting him help her off the stool. Something she was more than capable of doing herself.

Grabbing the file folder, she held it close to her chest, a good excuse to have her hands occupied for the walk.

"I am surprised you aren't keeping everything on a company tablet or laptop." Decker gestured toward the folder as they headed out onto the street.

"Oh." Frankie let out a sigh. "As a business owner, you might not like hearing this but I don't want it on the company servers. Not yet, anyway."

If this service worked…and it would… Frankie wanted to guarantee she had a place in the new division. Maybe that wasn't fair to Amelia, but she'd watched others take credit for her work when she was at the clothing design firm. They got promoted, and she got fired.

That wasn't happening again.

"Smart move." Decker led the way down and stopped outside a building that she would never have pegged as a jewelry store.

"Not planning to rat me out to Amelia?" She watched him enter a key, then a six-digit code above the lock, and heard the click.

"I kept my own paper records when I was clawing my way up the ladder in this business. My designs, my thoughts, the ideas I had. Makes sense." He put his hand on the door handle. "Ready?"

No.

"Lead the way."

"Just hold on one second." He needed to get the lights and figure out exactly how he was going to make this *magical*.

The word had floated out of his lips as he tried to come up with some reason for the two of them to spend more time together. This was a unique store, one that only upscale clients ever saw, but it was just a store.

Flipping the lights on, Decker walked back out to find Frankie standing in the center of the room. "I would never have known this was a jewelry store. Don't most stores have windows advertising their wares?" She winked as she walked over to one of the display cases.

"Most stores do. In fact this is the only Heughs Jewelry location that doesn't."

"So it's where the rich and famous shop." She looked up from the case, tapping her fingers on the glass. "What is the wildest demand you've ever had?"

That was a unique question. And one of the reasons it was so easy to fall for her. Most people asked things about the celebrities that wore his pieces.

They wanted the gossip. The cheeky details that were usually tied into nondisclosure agreements.

"I had a gentleman who wanted the exact same piece made for his wife and *both* his mistresses. Three emerald necklaces with matching earrings." Decker rolled his eyes. "Never mind that his wife preferred pearls, one mistress had a thing for pink diamonds and the other hated emeralds—something about them being bad luck."

"I think if your partner is giving two other women the exact same emerald necklace, then emeralds aren't the cause of any bad luck." Frankie let out a breath. "Did the women find out?"

"The wife knew. She returned the piece and picked out something more to her own liking and went on her way. Not sure about the first mistress, but the one who hated emeralds made him return it." Decker moved to the display case. "Maybe the other was happy enough with it? Technically the pieces are still here. Never managed to sell them." He pulled one of the emerald necklaces from the case, holding it up.

Frankie's nose wrinkled at the gawdy piece. "Of course it hasn't sold. The setting is off." She wandered over, her frown deepening the closer she got.

"What do you mean off?" He hadn't designed the piece. One of the junior assistants had handled the request. But the piece was fine enough. The large emerald in the center was surrounded by smaller emeralds and the chain was coated in more emeralds. Each piece was worth close to a hundred thousand pounds.

"The center emerald is diminished by the pieces around it." She tilted her head, her dark gaze rotating around the piece in his hands. "The emerald is supposed to be the centerpiece but other gems demand the eye, too, instead of fading into the glitter of the necklace. Right now the setting is fighting itself." She let out a soft chuckle. "That probably sounded ridiculous."

Decker looked at the piece. He hadn't designed it but it was exactly what the client had requested. That didn't mean Frankie wasn't 100 percent correct in her assessment. "No. It sounded like you were a designer. Did you design jewelry at the fashion house you worked for?"

The scoff that left her beautiful lips was deep and heartbreaking. "No. It was clothes and I was *only* an assistant."

"*Only* is an interesting way to label yourself." He put the emerald necklace back in the case. He'd rework the piece at some point, because Frankie was absolutely correct. A few changes and the necklaces would sell immediately.

She wandered over to the case of engagement rings. "Only is what I was. The designer got the credit. I was just there."

"Did you design any of their portfolio?" He already knew the answer. One did not describe themselves as *only* an assistant, unless they'd been told that while someone was stealing their work.

He'd seen it more than once in the world he worked in. Decker wasn't the primary designer these days. Hell, there were months where he didn't get anywhere near the tools of his craft. But when he was moving up, early in his career, more than one of his pieces had been labeled with someone else's name.

"I once stood in the crowd clapping as the partner of the first firm I worked at received an award for the piece I designed and crafted," he said. "My name was never mentioned. Never acknowledged. When I returned to work on Monday, not a single person on the development team told me good job." That was the real rub of it. Everyone knew.

And not one of his colleagues acknowledged his part in the success.

"But you weren't fired over it."

He barely heard the statement. And he saw her brush a tear off her cheek before pointing to the case of rings. "This whole case is diamond engagement rings, why? Diamonds aren't even that rare. It's all marketing."

She wanted to shift the topic. Decker understood, but there was one thing he needed her to know. "Just because a company couldn't see your worth doesn't mean it wasn't there."

When Frankie met his gaze, her eyes were clear. "I know. But it still stings. I can probably see the flaw in your necklace because I looked at so many designs in the six months I worked for them. But come on, why diamonds?"

"I mean there is a history, but I suspect the answer is because it is still what people think they should buy." He leaned over the counter. At least with the glass between them, he wasn't in danger of reaching for her.

"What they should do." She stuck her tongue out. "Why not pick a gemstone for its meaning? You could have an emerald stone, since it means harmony and romance. Or what about a garnet for passion?"

"Interesting perspective from a matchmaker." He understood her point. After all, humans assigned meaning to a whole host of things. Diamonds meant abundance. They were a status symbol. But the purpose of Andilet was to find a partner.

Decker wanted love. But that made him unique in his circle. The woman whose husband had two mistresses hadn't been angry at the turn her life had taken. She had been resigned…or maybe that was just the way Decker had read the situation. She'd come in and asked for a different necklace. They'd replaced it and she'd left a happy customer. Perhaps her husband's antics were no big deal to her.

"I'm not a matchmaker." Frankie smiled up at him. "Not really. I am a dating coach for one very specific client. In theory, I will lead a new division at Andilet, if I can get my client ready for the woman he wants."

I want you.

The words were stuck in the back of his throat.

"I walked in the first day and was told to *date* you."

He grabbed her hands as she made the air quotes around date. "What if I don't find a match in Andilet's client list?" That wasn't what he should say. The truth was he should have been honest the moment he found out about the company's scheme. Asked Frankie out and see if there was a path for them.

He could do it now, too. They were alone. This wasn't a date set up by the company. But the words stayed buried.

"Already losing faith in me?" She put out a fake pout. "Really, Decker."

"You know I'm not." He leaned a little closer.

She swallowed, then pursed her lips before pushing off the display case. "This is really interesting, Mr. Heughs, but what makes it magical?"

You.

He let out a chuckle. "I don't know."

"Decker!"

"I just wanted a few more minutes, Frankie. I enjoy your company." That wasn't even close to the full truth. He craved her company. Wanted so much more than the fake date coaching. "This is pretty cool, though." He walked to the back and flipped a few switches. The room was dark now, except for the one overhead light.

"Oh!"

Her exclamation was loud enough to carry to the back. At least he hadn't completely lied.

He slipped back into the darkened room. The jewelry sparkled in the cases, casting rainbows on the walls.

"It is." Frankie spun. "Almost like a movie."

"A movie?" He wasn't exactly sure what that meant.

"Please." Frankie strutted toward him. "If you are about to tell me you don't watch movies, and haven't seen any of the romantic comedies that were so popular when we were growing up—" She paused and shook her head. "You don't watch movies, do you, Decker?"

Her look of disappointment radiated through him. She wasn't wrong, though.

"This was my focus." The sparkly gems were the prize. He'd won it.

"That's so sad." Frankie wrapped her arms around herself. "I should get going." She went to the case and grabbed the file she'd brought with her. "Thank you, Decker. This was enlightening."

"Enlightening?" The word jabbed at him. "Meaning?"

She held her hand out; sparkles bounced off her as she tilted her head. Frankie glowed.

"I think part of the dating coach project needs to include talking to people about what they enjoy most. Not just hobbies—which I know you don't have—but likes and dislikes. Favorite foods, music, movies you can't stand and those you will buy a ticket to no matter how overdone the genre."

He didn't have any of that. He liked pub food. Enjoyed sitting on his balcony with coffee in the morning. Though he hadn't done it in years. But Decker had nothing to add to this unintended dress down.

She walked over to him, put a hand on his chest. "Don't frown." Her hand cupped his cheek for just a moment before she stepped back. "But I think finding those before finding a partner is incredibly important. If you don't know yourself, then how can you know what you want? So many of our clients are wildly successful, but if a person's only focus is work, what happens when work ends?"

"How could it end?" The question was out and if he thought the disappointment on her face over the movie comment stung, it was nothing compared to the way her features fell now.

"All work ends, Decker. Or it should. Most of the world works so they can maybe, one day, do their favorite things in life. Crochet all day. Grow the biggest garden. Ski. Sit in coffee shops and people watch. Write the novel they've always wanted to publish."

She took a deep breath. "Work is not life. It's not

what makes our limited time on this planet worth-while. It's a stepping stone to do what we want."

He'd never experienced a quiet so loud. The gems sparkled. But they just stared at each other.

Finally, she turned to the door. "Good night, Decker."

"Night, Frankie."

She was gone. The gems still sparkled but the magic left with her.

CHAPTER SIX

FOUR DAYS. Four silent days.

Decker looked at his phone. Silent wasn't actually true. He'd gotten texts from Frankie's work phone. Not the number she'd given him that first night.

Can we meet up?

I am sorry. I didn't mean to upset you.

I understand if you want to meet with someone else.

That last one stung the hardest. Because he didn't want to meet with anyone else. He wanted her.

He also knew that she was right. He didn't know himself, not really. He'd looked over the pathetic profile he'd built for Andilet. It didn't even read as a dating profile.

He was work.

That was all that defined him. He'd signed up for Andilet's services to make his mother happy.

And thrown himself into it in the last six months because of her worsening symptoms. The dementia's progression meant he had little time left to fulfill that goal.

Not the best reason to find a spouse.

I've heard worse.

That was the mental repetition he'd used to explain his reasons. But it was so hollow now.

The film's credits rolled and Decker struck art film from his list. He understood the premise. Understood that the creator was making a statement. But he hadn't cared for the three he'd watched. So that meant art film and horror were now off the list of movies he liked.

Documentaries and romantic comedies were fighting for the top spot and superhero films were pulling in a surprising third. Maybe it wasn't much, but he'd taken Frankie's words to heart.

If he was going to be a partner, he needed to be more than a jewelry designer and company CEO. After all, an impressive résumé wasn't the best way to offer yourself to another.

It would be enough for some women.

That was his father's nasty tone ringing in his mind. That voice wasn't wrong, either. There were people who'd happily accept a union crystalized out of shared social standing.

His father had had a few relationships like that. Once upon a time Decker had planned to act as his groomsman. Others might have considered it cute or sweet for his father's not-quite-teenage son to stand beside him. The truth was there was no one else. His fiancée, Margot, had picked everything out for the wedding—and promptly called it off the second his father lost his company.

And his father mourned the business. Not the runaway bride.

Decker looked at his watch. He had just enough time to make it to Andilet before they closed up for the day. His stomach alternated between excitement and a desire to toss the popcorn he'd popped for the films. Now or never.

The tube was crowded with people getting an early start on their Thursday evenings. He was going against the flow into downtown. Three stops. Two stops. One.

The crowd waiting to get in was far larger than the few stepping out of it. He looked at the faces as he stepped out. No sign of Frankie. Not that he expected her. She was figuring out the dating coach side for Andilet. She'd be working until closing, making a good impression.

Or maybe I'm projecting how I'd act onto her.

He stepped up to the building and pushed the door open. The receptionist turned in her chair, her eyes widening as she grabbed the desk—probably pushing a button alerting Amelia that an important client was here.

As if on cue, Amelia stepped from her office. "Mr. Heughs."

"Is Frankie here?" He wasn't having this conversation without her.

Amelia nodded and held the door open to her office. Frankie was sitting in the chair. Her eyes widened as he stepped through the door.

"Were you discussing the dating coach services?" He slid into the seat next to Frankie. Lemon, cinnamon and sunshine hit his nose. Man, he'd missed her.

"Yes. I was outlining my plans. But Amelia—"

"Has some concerns." Amelia slid behind her desk. "But since you are here, perhaps you can allay some of them."

Decker shifted in his seat. "I think Frankie will do great as the lead of the service. She is brilliant and more than capable of delivering the words a client needs to hear."

Frankie took a deep breath, her dark gaze shifting to him for a second before she focused on Amelia.

"But I've come to end my services."

Frankie bit her lip, then immediately let it go. "I should let you and Amelia—"

"Stay. Because I want to be very clear that I am ending this because of Frankie." Decker bowed his head. "She made me realize things about myself. Made me step back and examine what I really want. She will make an excellent dating coach."

"One so good you're leaving." The words under Frankie's breath were loud enough for him. But

Amelia was either too focused on Decker to notice or ignoring it for later.

"Not sure a dating coach telling you that you aren't ready to enter a full partnership is a great sign." Amelia leaned back in her chair.

"I am. After all, you have a success rate of one hundred percent—minus me—of people walking down the aisle."

Amelia raised her chin. "Yes. We do."

So she really wasn't counting failures that happened when the company stepped out of the process.

"And how many of those couples failed to meet at the altar, and of the ones that did, how many are still together after five years?" Decker had looked into the few people he knew set up by Andilet. Using the matchmaking service was what many of the wealthy business owners and even some of the untitled aristocracy did. But one did not brag about it.

Still, it was easy enough to deduce. He knew of fifteen couples in the last ten years. Only two were still married. One very happily. They were the envy of far too many. The other was still together on paper only. They attended a few of the same events, but each had at least one affair partner on the side.

Decker tilted his head. "Should I give the metrics I know? I know you are tracking it. This firm is too data driven not to."

"Amelia?" Frankie's gaze was focused on her boss.

"It's a known issue with the clientele." Amelia cleared her throat. Apparently that was all the confirmation he was going to get.

"It isn't a problem—yet." He was a businessman at heart. There was a glaring issue with Andilet's operation. A generation ago, people might have chosen to stay unhappy. But divorce was common enough now that most people wouldn't avoid it simply for fear of society's wagging tongues.

"You are officially canceling? Is there nothing I can do? We can give you some free months. Or—" So they were back to the dating service. Anything to avoid the topic at hand.

But he wasn't done quite yet. "With the coaching service, you might lose a client here and there, but your success rate, the real success rate, will go up. And you will get more than just the empty words on that horridly long form you send everyone."

"Not that you filled it out." This time, Frankie's words were clearly said for the room.

"Not that I filled it out." Decker winked. She was so close. There were so many things he wanted to say to her. So many things he planned to say to her. But not with Amelia present.

He suddenly wanted this over. He'd come to make sure Amelia knew his personal thoughts. And to make sure she didn't punish Frankie for what was coming. The woman had pushed her newest employee to the brink in many ways. Ways that Frankie could take to the employment council, if she chose.

And yet she'd taken each request and turned it into something that had the capacity to make a real impact for Andilet. Frankie was a genius. If Amelia let her loose, there was no telling how far she'd go.

"I am not requesting a refund, Amelia." The woman's shoulders relaxed immediately.

All this bluster and commentary over the large sum of money that the contract said he was owed.

Decker shook his head, "Your team worked hard on finding the right person. My failings in that regard are my failings alone."

"All right, then." Amelia nodded and passed over a tablet. "You need to sign the cancellation. If you find yourself in need of our services again—"

"I hope I don't." Decker coughed. He hadn't meant to say that—out loud. Didn't mean it wasn't true. If he got his dream, then he was never signing up for another service. "I just mean, maybe I… umm…will have better luck on my own."

Frankie shot him a look that he was pretty sure was supposed to mean, *What the heck?* But she didn't say anything. That was fine.

The next stage of this plan started once she was off work.

Decker was gone. There was no reason for Frankie to text him. No dates to schedule. Nothing.

He'd marched in today…and marched out less than twenty minutes later.

That was the plan. At least it was supposed to be. You got someone ready to meet a potential spouse, or to accept they weren't ready for Andilet's services. Frankie had done a good job.

And it means he's gone.

She grabbed her purse as her stomach twisted. Frankie ordered her body to relax as she looked at the tiny office. *Her* tiny office.

Not a cubicle. Not an assistant matchmaker. Lead of a fledgling service in an established, but faltering, business. How her fortunes had shifted since he dumped coffee on those painful yellow shoes. Decker was gone but she was in charge of the dating coach launch.

Because Amelia thinks it will fail.

There was that stomach twist again. Frankie closed her eyes and took a deep breath. She could prove Amelia wrong.

Never proved anyone wrong before. I just left.

Her mind was as intent as her body on reminding Frankie of her faults. Each said in the grating tone of her mother. Like Frankie wasn't aware of the choices she'd made since leaving her parents' home.

This was hers. Hers. Maybe Amelia was convinced it would fail. That was fine. Frankie was going to see it through.

My first client walked away from dating altogether.

So she was starting with a zero percent success rate. Tomorrow was a fresh day. Tomorrow that average went up. Tomorrow.

She flipped out the light and looked at her feet. Her toes ached from the heels she'd chosen this morning. She wanted a pint and a few minutes in a loud pub to drown out the thoughts in her mind.

And she wanted to grab the tube, head home, cry under a scalding shower, put on comfy pants and crochet until her mind worked through all the emotions about Decker vanishing from her life.

I don't have emotions.

Now I'm lying to myself.

And arguing with myself.

All right, that settled it. A pub. Because if she was alone with her thoughts, they'd work overtime to drive her mad.

"Night, Frankie. Congrats." Patricia was gathering her things from behind the reception desk. "And good luck. You are going to need it."

Frankie bit her lip and looked toward Amelia's door. It was closed.

"*Because,*" Patricia redirected Frankie's attention, "the clients need more work than any of them are willing to admit."

Frankie grinned. "You don't say."

They giggled as they headed for the door. "I'm going to stop at the pub on the corner. Want to join me?"

Patricia patted Frankie's shoulder as she offered

what anyone could tell was a no-thank-you smile. "Normally, I would say yes, but it's my anniversary." She held up her ring finger. "Two years."

"Congrats." The ring sparkled on her hand. That was the perfect reason to skip a noisy pub. If Frankie had someone to run home to, to discuss the day with, she wouldn't dread her tiny flat so much. "That is a gorgeous ring."

"It's not a Heughs piece." Patricia looked at the tiny diamond. "But when Sally put it in the cake at dinner three years ago—" she swallowed as happy tears clouded her blue eyes "—I would have said yes to anything. She is my world."

"When it's the right person, a ring from a gumball machine is more than enough." When visiting the crown jewels with her mother, Frankie hadn't thought much of the opulence. The small ring her father bought her mother when they were grad students living in a flat with three other flat mates was prettier than all the jewels.

Her mother never took it off. Because, despite all her faults, she loved Frankie's father. Rings were simply a symbol.

Patricia pulled open the door and Frankie followed her. "Don't let the clients hear you say that."

If Frankie was good at her job, maybe some of the clients at Andilet might be more interested in the person offering forever than the ring in the box.

"Don't let them hear you say what?" Decker was leaning against the lamppost.

"What are you doing here?" It was a good thing she'd already been sitting when he'd strutted in and ended his contract, because she was certain her legs would have given out. Then he'd started defending her dating coach project.

A project she hadn't even really wanted a week ago, still wasn't sure she wanted, but was oddly protective of.

She'd gripped the arms of the chair to make sure she didn't reach out to him. He'd left and she'd used the few minutes left in the workday to try to start getting used to the fact that he was gone.

A fact that shouldn't bother her about a client.

Now he was casually hanging outside her office. Looking comfortable as hell while her insides were ripping apart.

"Frankie wanted to go to the pub, but I have to meet my wife for an anniversary dinner. You should go with her." Patricia offered a feisty wave as she darted toward the tube entrance.

"The pub? I could go for a pint." Decker straightened. "Want company?"

Pain shot through Frankie's bottom lip and she released her teeth's grip on it. At least that had kept her from screaming *yes*. Patricia was going to pay for abandoning her with him tomorrow.

"I was only grabbing one and then heading home. You don't have to come. I can just head on. My yarn is calling already. I can get into comfy trousers. I am sure you have very important things to do." Things that do not include hanging by a lamppost.

"That was a lot of words, Frankie." Decker crossed his arms but he didn't step away from the lamppost. "If you want to go home, that is fine."

She didn't want to. Not now. And that was the problem.

"Why are you here?" She wanted him to say *for you.* Wanted him to ask her out. To say maybe the fake dates had felt too real to him, too.

"I asked a question first. You tell me what Patricia meant when she said *don't let the clients hear you say that* and I'll tell you why I'm out here." He held out a hand for a shake.

A handshake. Wow. Mood-killer. But a good reminder that Decker was a *former* Andilet client.

She looked at it but didn't shake it. It was petty, but if she touched him, the heat she felt any time she was around him would explode. And a man interested in a woman did not offer handshakes.

"We were talking about rings. She said her engagement ring wasn't a Heughs ring but that she'd have said yes to anything when her wife proposed. I commented that maybe if the dating coach idea works out, the clients will realize that when it's the right person, a gumball machine ring is more than enough."

Decker playfully hung his mouth open while dramatically throwing the hand he'd offered for a shake over his forehead. "Francesca, are you trying to drive my company out of business?"

The giggle was on her lips before she could do anything else. "Decker." His deep laughter mixed with hers and more than a few heads turned their direction.

These were the moments she'd craved. The silly, fun moments when the world blended into the background. When it was possible to believe that, despite the unusual start to their story, it might be a fairy tale, after all.

Except fairy tales were fictional for a reason. The original stories were warnings: Don't step out of place. Don't follow strangers. Don't fall in love with people outside your station.

That final thought pulled the laughter from her chest. Frankie pushed his shoulder without thinking, hating and loving the fleeting connection. Why did she have such a hard time not reaching for him? "Don't worry, Decker. I think, even if the clients don't care what the ring looks like, they will still seek out your wares."

"Oh. Good. Then I don't have to worry that Andilet is seeking the demise of my business." He gave her a wink and tilted his head down the street. "Ready for that pint?"

"You didn't answer my question." She put her hands on her hips, raising a brow. It was a playful gesture, but she meant it. She wanted, needed, to know why he was standing outside Andilet.

Decker's half grin as he leaned toward her sent shock waves down her spine. Damn, now that he wasn't a client, her body didn't even bother clamping down on its reaction to him.

"For you, of course."

The world danced, or maybe it was just the heat coating her skin. "For me?"

He leaned just a little closer, his soft scent invading her senses. She was already having trouble catching her breath and now the cinnamon musk complicated her breathing.

"Of course. I wanted to make sure Amelia didn't can you after I laid everything out."

"Of course." Frankie hoped the disappointment heating her cheeks wasn't obvious. "Nope. I have my own small office. Tiny, really. But mine."

He held out a hand, "Ready for the pint?"

Frankie took it, not really thinking through the motion. Her heart was acting because her brain refused to function. He pulled it through his arm, linking them together.

The silence spoke volumes as they took the short walk to the pub. At least the din of conversation in the pub was clear before the door even opened. There'd be little opportunity to discuss much. Though she doubted her brain would silence in all the noise.

"I'll grab the pints; you find us some seats. First round is mine." Decker let her go and headed to the bar.

Frankie let out a sigh. She should have gone home. Had a long cry and pulled herself together. This was a crush. Crushes were called that because they were fleeting, but also because they turned your heart to pulp.

At least for a minute.

Instead of finding a way to catch him before he ordered, Frankie headed to the small empty table she saw. One pint. Let her heart say goodbye and then take herself home.

"Good get." Decker slid into the chair opposite her. "This is the third time we've been in a pub." His giant grin was so at odds with the pressure in her chest.

"I guess so." Frankie held up her pint and took a deep sip. She didn't really count the first one. They'd gone to the pub under false pretensions. At least she had. The second night, well, that night she thought he might kiss her and gone home not quite understanding what was going on.

Tonight. Tonight was goodbye.

"So you are now the person in charge of the dating coach service. That is great, Frankie." He raised his pint. "To new beginnings."

Work talk. That was safe enough. "New beginnings."

"What's the first thing you're doing?" Decker set his beer down, leaned his elbows on the table and his head on his hands.

"Decorating. I'm sure Amelia will judge that.

The matchmaking office is refined. Mine won't be." That was something she felt strongly about.

"What does that mean?" Decker's gaze was rooted to her, like he was genuinely interested in what she had to say.

"Everyone lies about themselves in the early days of dating."

"Like saying you're a date when you're actually a spy gathering ammunition?" Decker winked.

Heat drove up her neck. He might be all right with it, or maybe he was covering well, but that didn't change the facts. "Usually it's not that deceptive. Sorry, again."

"Best thing that ever happened to me."

She wasn't sure about that. "*Lying* is too strong a word, maybe. It's that you're putting on your best face. You're talking about books or movies, and maybe overselling how much you like the classics so you seem like a connoisseur."

"And you certainly aren't saying anything about how you just drop your dirty socks in a pile by the door."

She giggled. "Right. And don't drop dirty socks by the door, Decker. You are in your thirties."

He shook his head, "Not me. My stepfather. My mom still yells at him about it. He's gotten better but that is still his first impulse. She once told him that if she'd known, she'd never have fallen for him." He let out a sigh; his gaze shifting behind Frankie.

"Yeah. Things like that. I want my office to have a personal feel. A place where people can be themselves. I plan to hang some succulents and bring in the knitted highland cow I made last month. Show off a little bit of myself, so they feel comfortable telling me about themselves."

"Wow." Decker leaned back in his chair and crossed his arms. "You've thought this all through."

"Dating coach wasn't on my career radar, but once you suggested it, I ran with it. In a weird way, I will owe you my career if this works."

"No." Decker shook his head, "*When* it works, it will be you. All you, Frankie."

She needed to go. Needed to close whatever chapter this was. "Thank you for coming with me tonight, Decker. I appreciate it. But as you can see, I am fine. Amelia didn't scream at me or fire me or anything dramatic. I really hope you find what you're looking for."

Frankie stood. She smiled as she stepped past him. And kept moving. That was as good a good-bye speech as she was going to give.

The evening air was fresh as she stepped onto the street. Time to go home. Have that cry and figure out tomorrow.

"Frankie!" Decker's call as she'd nearly hit the entrance to the tube was too much. She'd said goodbye. Eloquently.

He was panting as she turned around. "I had to close…close out the tab."

"Tab? They don't do tabs unless you order food."

"I know the owner."

Of course he did.

Decker put a hand on his hip. "Give me one sec."

She heard the tube rumble below; she wasn't making this one, anyway. "What, Decker?"

"I lied." He straightened but was still breathing fast.

"You don't know the pub owner?" Frankie moved so a businessman could race past her.

"I wasn't waiting to make sure Amelia wasn't a pain to you. I was waiting…" He sucked in another round of air.

The pause was the longest she'd ever experienced.

"I know it was fake. I know the dates were set up by the agency to figure me out. I know all that." Decker rocked on his heels. "But I was waiting to see if by any chance you might think there were real sparks. Real moments. Things that were just the two of us. Not Francesca from Andilet and Decker who can't make a match work."

She'd always rolled her eyes when the romance novels she loved talked about letting out a breath you didn't know you were holding. But her lungs were burning. "Yes, there were real moments."

"Go on a date with me, Frankie. A real one. Just us. Tomorrow? I'll set everything up."

"Like the ghost hunt?" She hated to bring that

up, but the one time he'd arranged a date, even a fake one, he'd left her standing on her own.

"Nope. My former dating coach reminded me, a lot actually, that I should be present." He reached for her hand and she let him take it. "And I want to be present, Frankie. So, I am going to text you—your phone, not the company one—a location and time."

"It's a date." Frankie grinned as he pulled her hand to his lips.

"Get going, I don't want to keep you from the next train. Tomorrow, Frankie." He squeezed her hand one more time, then dropped it and stepped back.

"Tomorrow."

CHAPTER SEVEN

"HAVE FUN ON your date." Patricia clicked her tongue as they stepped out of the office the next day.

"Date? I never said I had a date." In fact she'd kept that very quiet. Frankie might feel like she was walking on air, but she wasn't ready to let the office know.

Specifically Amelia.

"Come on, *Francesca*!" Patricia wagged her finger. "He was waiting for you. You two have *it*."

"It?" Frankie looked at her watch. She was in exactly no danger of being late for their meetup, but she'd found herself counting down the time all day. An hour and twelve minutes to go.

More than enough time to make it to the location he'd texted her.

"The spark, Frankie. I have it with my wife. I am not saying it's a forever thing, but the chemistry is plain as hell for anyone looking. Now," Patricia looked at her bare wrist, "time to get going."

"You aren't wearing a watch." Frankie stuck out her tongue, then waved and headed for the tube.

She wasn't sure what they were doing, but Decker had seemed pretty excited in the texts he'd sent last night.

As she got closer and closer to the address, Frankie was more and more aware that she was in danger of arriving painfully early.

There hadn't been enough time to run home between work and the date. And Decker had said it was a low-key event. Still, she'd worn the bright yellow dress he'd seen her in first. But now there was twenty minutes before she was even supposed to meet up with him.

"You're early."

Frankie spun and shook her head. "*So* are you." He'd come early, too. There was no way this man, the one so focused on his business, was this early. And yet here he was.

Dressed in loose slacks and a blue top that brought out the jeweled tones in his eyes. He was scrumptious. And now, she was allowed to fully enjoy the moment.

"I love that dress." Decker held out his hand, this time their fingers wrapped together as he pulled her close. "You are sunshine."

She leaned her head against his shoulder for just a second.

"No need to pull back now." Decker dropped her hand and put his arm around her waist.

"True." This should not feel so natural. She laid her head back on his shoulder. Frankie was not usually handsy on a first date, but it wasn't a true first date. "So where are we going? I will admit I had not pegged you as one to book a date on Tottenham Court Road."

"Well, this area has a little bit of everything, and—" he opened a door "—here we are."

A young woman was sitting behind a desk covered in board games. Life-size game pieces stood in the corner and smaller pieces were tacked to the walls. She could have been given a hundred guesses as to what was behind the door they'd just walked through and never guessed this.

"Welcome, Mr. Heughs. Your table is ready."

"We are early." Frankie looked around. She wasn't sure what a table was in a location like this, but she'd worked in the service industry. Showing up twenty minutes early to a reservation was a no-no.

"We're the only ones here tonight, Frankie. And we will not rush the chef, but we can start with a cocktail." He squeezed her before releasing her and pulling out her chair.

"What kind of place is this?" Frankie ran her hand over the board game embedded in the resin tabletop.

"A first-date-experience-you-will-never-forget-kinda place." Decker handed her the drink menu.

"They're all board game–related." She couldn't contain her giggles as she read the ingredients for The Boardwalk, Luxury Tax and Go To Jail!

"Of course." Decker gestured to the room around them. "This whole place is a giant board game. When we finish our three-course meal, we get to play a life-size escape room themed around a board game."

Her mouth was hanging open. A board game escape room?

"Now, what cocktail would you like?" Decker leaned over. "Because I am going to get the Go To Jail."

"I don't know. I didn't play a lot of board games growing up. I don't understand all the references. My parents banned board games after a terrible Monopoly session when Catalina and I were nine and seven."

His eyes widened. "Umm—"

"We are playing the Monopoly escape room, aren't we?"

Decker raised his hands. "It is their most popular."

She reached for his hand, enjoying how their fingers locked together automatically. "As long as you don't cheat like my sister, then there should be no problem."

"Your sister cheated?"

Frankie shrugged. "Catalina told my parents she didn't. They believed her. But I was going to win." That was the part that still cut her soul whenever this family story was brought up.

It was silly to care about a game from two decades ago. "Catalina and I were always competing."

"And she always won." Decker rolled his thumb across her wrist.

"Obvious, isn't it." Frankie's parents had encouraged the competitiveness…as long as it wasn't ruining their quiet evenings. Sisterly disagreements were ruled off-limits.

Like children never fought with each other.

"So, do I need to worry about you going toe to toe with me in the escape room?" Decker playfully raised a brow.

"No." She rolled her eyes, good-humoredly. "I'm not the competitive one." The game Catalina had gotten upset about was the last one Frankie had cared about. Catalina's childhood room, meanwhile, was filled with trophies and certificates.

Frankie's held no trophies. When school award ceremonies arrived, her parents had never bothered to come. After all, she wouldn't be getting anything.

"Besides, I've never done an escape room, but aren't we supposed to work together?" She was looking forward to it. Looking forward to them figuring out the puzzles and laughing.

"I haven't done one, either. But I think that is the general idea." Decker pulled back as the waitress brought their cocktails.

Frankie's was bright blue and had a little umbrella that she immediately grabbed and spun. "If you've never done an escape room, why did you choose this for our first date?"

If he'd never done this before, then that meant they were making wholly new memories. No harking back to a common fun date he'd shared with others. This was theirs. Only theirs.

Color bloomed in his cheeks as he grabbed his far less vibrant drink and hung his head just a tad. "Honestly?"

"Yes." Frankie took a sip of her drink and bit back a grimace. "Wow. That is sweet."

"Want to switch?"

"Maybe, but I feel like you're putting off telling me why I am sitting in a themed board game escape room that also has three-course meals." She gestured for him to tell the story.

"I legit did an internet search for the best dates in London and found a list of like a hundred things. Pretty overwhelming, actually." Decker laughed. "This one had great reviews."

"A listicle. You used a listicle to pick out our date." At least he hadn't done what she'd first suspected when he'd hung his head: asked his personal assistant to schedule it.

"I wanted to make a statement for you, Frankie. Do something different. Fun and unique." He gestured to the room.

"Unique it is." She lifted her glass. "To unique first dates."

They clinked the glasses and took another sip.

And there was no way for her to hide her grimace. The name was fun, but the drink was basically pure sugar.

"Here." Decker passed her his drink. "The Go To Jail isn't sweet." He grabbed hers and took a sip. "Yum. I don't know why you don't like this, but I am going to enjoy every bit of it."

"Have we tried this?" Frankie ran over to the large rocking horse piece and looked for some hidden box or a lever. Anything that might harbor the last key for them to escape the room.

"We did. But maybe there's something we missed?"

Frankie put her hands on her hips as she looked at him. "Do you really think that?"

This woman was competitive. Maybe she'd buried it in the depths of her soul in search of family harmony. But she craved the win—and the clock was ticking down.

"No." Decker blew out a breath and looked around the room. They'd solved four puzzles, each producing a key to a new room. Now they were in the final space, with an exit directly in front of them. And no indicator on how they were to "break free."

"You've looked all over this room. I've searched, there is no puzzle." Frankie walked over to him. Her gaze floated from object to object in the room.

"The door says this way to the exit." Decker looked at it. "Any chance we just open it?"

"It can't be that easy." Frankie hit her hip against his. "Each of the other doors said this way to the next room, and we found keys to unlock all of them."

Decker wrapped his arm around her waist. "One minute left."

Frankie bit her lip. "What do we do?"

Decker pulled her closer. "We wait for the alarm to tell us we failed."

Her bottom lip trembled.

"Hey, this is supposed to be fun. I have had the best time, minus your drink. It *was* too sweet." He winked.

"I knew it." Frankie kissed his cheek. "This was fun."

The buzzer on the wall went off and her shoulders fell a little. Decker raised her chin with his finger. "I wouldn't change a thing about tonight."

"Not even beating the dumb puzzle?"

He ran his fingers over her cheek. "Nope. I am ending this experience exactly where I want to. With you in my arms." He pressed his lips to her forehead.

His soul ached to lower his lips to hers, but the game managers were monitoring them via cameras, and he didn't want strangers watching their first kiss on a screen. That moment would be just for them.

"Excuse me." The voice from the speaker hovered

over them. "The answer was just going through the door. It's unlocked."

Man. Frankie was going to blame herself now.

"Not a big deal, sweetie."

"You were right, though." Frankie sighed as she stepped out of his arms.

They needed to go, but he hated the empty feeling she left.

"It's a trick. It's supposed to trick you." He opened the door. This was going to bother her. The fun exercise wasn't supposed to put a frown on her lips.

"But you were right and I shut you down. I got competitive and—"

"And nothing." Decker put a finger over her lips. "You are allowed to be competitive, Frankie. Allowed to chase what you want."

They stepped into the foyer. The attendee was holding a board that said I Failed to Break Out. "Ready for the picture?"

Decker grabbed it. "We can skip it, Frankie."

"No. May as well finish off the experience." Frankie started to reach for the other side of the sign, but Decker pulled it back.

"I am holding it, and you are wrapping your arms around me." He raised his eyebrows a few times. If she balked at holding him, he wouldn't push, but the sign bothered her and he wanted a picture. A fun picture.

Frankie giggled and put her arms around his

shoulders. "I can't believe you want a picture of this failure."

"Not a failure." Decker pressed his lips to her forehead. "I have you wrapping your arms around me. That is the pinnacle of success."

"You would know about success." Frankie kissed his cheek as the attendant snapped the photo. Decker would be framing that.

But there was an undertone in her comment that sent a chill down his spine. He was successful, by society's standards. Frankie had job-hopped, but that didn't mean she wasn't successful, too.

She'd remade herself over and over again. Not everyone had that strength. Hell, he'd only stepped into his father's role. Made it his own, but still.

"Frankie—"

She bounced from his arm over to the counter. "You buying the photo?"

He recognized a topic shift. Besides, this wasn't the place to have that conversation.

"Of course." He pulled out his card and waved hers away as she reached for her wallet. "Nope, tonight is my treat completely. This was the most fun I've had in forever."

"More fun than mudlarking?" Frankie chuckled at the face he made while they waited for the attendant to print out their photo. "I enjoyed my time with you, but we both know looking through trash on the river will never be my favorite activity."

"Historic trash." Frankie pursed her lips as the lie slipped through. Yes, there were historical finds but there was very real modern trash washing up on those shores, too.

He tapped her nose, "And I am pretty sure you were miserable like me."

Frankie leaned against the counter. "I was but not because of the mudlarking." Her eyes widened at her—clearly accidental—admission.

"Oh, no. You can't stop there." He grabbed the picture from the attendant and then Frankie's hand. He was letting the comment about competitiveness drop but not this one.

He opened the door and they exited the quiet into the bustle of the London evening. "*Frankie*, why were you so miserable?"

She stuck her tongue out. "I don't think you need any more of an ego boost."

"Sure I do." He squeezed her waist. He'd spent so much of tonight touching her. And she hadn't pulled back once. They were on a date, a real one.

Frankie leaned her head against his. "If you'd continued with the dating coach service, I'd planned to do a Jack the Ripper tour, and a night-time venture to the Tower where they cover more gruesome history than the daytime tour."

"Gruesome." He tilted his head. "I know you were excited about the ghost tour, and then a little squeamish about going into the tunnels. No judgment. But do you have any actual interest in those activities?"

"No." Frankie stopped in front of an oddities shop that was already closed.

The glow of the streetlamps hit her cheeks. She was so beautiful.

"The Ripper tours are focused on the enigma; they rarely address the women as anything more than sex workers. The insinuation being that they deserved what happened because they were *less than*. And execution stories are mostly histories of those on the wrong side of a king or religious organization. Add in telling the tales at night…no, thank you." She pointed to a small heart-shaped stone in the corner of the display. "That is so pretty. I bet in the sunlight it sparkles in the window."

Decker made a mental note of the object. He'd come back for it. "Were you choosing very uncomfortable locations to ensure you didn't end up in my arms?"

Frankie grinned as she looked away from the window. "You're very smart, Decker."

"I know." He pulled her close.

"I liked you that first date. I wasn't supposed to and then when we went geocaching and you touched me, I…" She looked at him, running a hand over his cheek. "I wanted places that were the opposite of sexy. I wanted distance."

"There is no distance now." His husky tone spun

into the evening and his soul sang as her fingers stroked his face.

"Nope. So there really is only one question." She raised a brow.

"You going to let me in on it?" His fingers ran along her waist. He caught every single hitch of her breath. She was driving him mad with the gentle strokes on his cheek, but he was affecting her, too.

"Are you going to kiss me, Decker?"

The only answer he gave was the dip of his head. Their lips connected and the noise of the London streets disappeared. This was as close to heaven as he'd ever been.

Decker had bought companies from his enemies, rebuilt a corporate empire and those successes paled when this woman was in his arms.

He pulled her a little closer.

"Hey! Get a room!"

Frankie pressed her lips to his for a moment longer before stepping back. "I haven't been told to get a room since I was a teenager snogging on the tube." She brushed her lips against his. "Totally worth it."

"Absolutely." Decker wrapped his arm around her shoulder. "Want to spend a little more time window-shopping, or are you ready to head home?" He didn't want to call it a night, but if she was ready...

"I could look at a few more shop windows.

Maybe see if we can get yelled at on each block for kissing?" She playfully pulled him along.

Kissing her on every block… There was no better way to end an evening.

CHAPTER EIGHT

DECKER SMOOTHED HIS shirt as he walked up the stairs toward Frankie's flat. He'd seen her less than twenty-four hours ago and it felt like forever. And this date was different.

Meeting a date out was a good plan for the first few encounters. Picking a date up at her place was a new step. It involved trust and the hope that a relationship was developing. Frankie was letting him in.

And there is no way I am messing this up.

He ran his hands along his shirt one more time. Like the action could smooth any wrinkles the seven flights of stairs caused.

The door of the apartment opened before he'd even raised a hand. Frankie let out an adorable squeak as she nearly ran into him.

"Were you looking out the peep hole for me?" No one had ever waited for him like that.

"No." Frankie took a deep breath. "Finding you right outside my flat took my breath away—and not in the let-your-ego-bloom kind of way."

She kissed his cheek. "The complex just sent a memo that the lift is out."

"Yes, it certainly is." Decker pointed to the stairs. "It was quite the climb."

"Sorry. I was heading out so I could meet you on the first floor." Frankie looked back at her flat. "Do you mind if I grab a different bag? I was in the middle of changing it out when the note came through."

"Of course not." He shrugged. "Want me to wait out here?" He wanted to see Frankie's place but he was not going to invade her sanctuary without an invitation.

"No. You can come in. It's tiny, fair warning." She pulled back and headed to the bed where the yellow bag she'd worn last time with the yellow dress was dumped on the bed.

Tiny was an understatement. The studio apartment couldn't be more than four hundred square feet from the door to the opposite wall. But she'd made it her own. An impressive feat with such a small accommodation.

She'd created a curtain dividing the living space from her bed, one that was pushed back right now, but gave the air of separated space. There was a light blue sofa printed with roses and a yarn basket sitting in the corner of it. The TV was jammed in the corner with dozens of crocheted animals sitting on top.

During university he'd lived in a studio apartment, one maybe a bit bigger than this one. But he'd put up no decorations. It was a space he'd slept in, not one he lived in. An argument his mother made about his current, much larger, flat, too.

She'd complained more than once that it looked like the showroom for his luxury apartment community rather than a home he owned.

"All right." Frankie slid the few leftovers on the bed into the yellow purse and moved it to the wardrobe. Then she grabbed her blue bag and slung it over her shoulder. "Ready to walk back down those stairs?"

He pulled her into his arms when she got closer. "In one moment." He ran his hand up her back. "We kissed last night."

"And got yelled at on nearly every block."

"Nearly." No one had bothered them on the last one. Her grin was intoxicating. "We were interrupted many times."

"We were." Frankie wrapped her arms around his neck. "My place is tiny, but I don't have any roommates that will walk in and tell us to get a room."

Siren, that was the only way to describe her. Her lips skimmed his. Such a fiery touch for so little contact.

"Kiss me, Decker."

His hands wrapped around her waist, closing the tiny space between them. His lips captured hers as his fingers traced small circles on her back.

She melted into him. Time stood still as they teased each other. He memorized every soft moan, recreated every caress that made her shudder.

He'd stand here all night. Kiss her until the sun rose.

"Decker." Her voice was husky, desire-soaked.

"Frankie." He took in the dark gaze, the perfect lips.

"What are we doing tonight?"

Fair question. He'd had a whole plan. Still had the plan, he just needed his mind to recalibrate.

"Jewelry. We are doing jewelry."

"Doing jewelry?" Frankie raised a brow. "Your brain short-circuit?"

"Who is looking to grow their ego now?" He pressed his lips to her cheek.

"My ego is perfectly fine." She giggled as she grabbed his hand, pulling him through her door. "Come on, you can have a few minutes to recover while we make our way down the stairs."

At least going down the stairs was far easier than climbing them, particularly with Frankie's hand in his. The sun was high in the sky as they exited.

"Now—" Frankie turned to him "—what are we doing? Jewelry?"

Decker chuckled. "My head is a little clearer." He pulled his cell phone out and pressed a few buttons. In a minute their ride pulled up to the curb.

He opened the door, Frankie slid in and the car took off as soon as he closed it behind him.

"Okay, this I could get used to." Frankie leaned against the leather seats. "No unwelcome stares, lewd comments or men that stand just a little too close."

The words were horrid but said with no malice, just a standard statement from a woman who'd outlined a likely daily experience.

"Anytime you want a ride, you let me know." He scooted closer.

"Oh, I was just making a statement." Frankie waved away the offer. "Now, where are we going?"

"Heughs Jewelry headquarters."

Her brows tightened and it wasn't quite a frown on her lips, but he could see the confusion.

"Not to work, Frankie. I want to show you something."

"Something magical?" She pursed her lips but it didn't quite contain the giggle.

"I hope so. And this time, I have an actual plan besides just trying to extend an evening with you." He put his hand on her knee. The purple dress she had on today was not a workplace dress. The strapless contraption had a cutout just below her breasts. Two thin straps of clothing connected the bust to the short skirt and the open back. The piece was divine.

"I love the yellow dress. But this one." Decker ran his thumb over her knee, enjoying the slight darkening in her cheeks.

"First time I've worn it. I designed it. Last piece

I made—no room for a sewing machine in my flat." She ran her hands along the fabric. "It's actually the dress that got me fired."

Decker didn't have any words. How could anyone look at this design work and cut the talent loose?

"It's a lightweight fabric and wash and wear. So not high-end." She sighed and glanced out the window. "But I think it's lovely, even if you can throw it in a washing machine instead of dry cleaning."

So the answer was she'd created something anyone might own. There were a few jewelry stores that only catered to clients who would spend at least fifty thousand pounds on pieces. Heughs had a few places, like the one he'd showed Frankie, that were invitation-only locations.

But he also had a line of jewelry that was specifically priced for anyone to own. That was something his father would not have approved of. But he'd found that he made as much money on it as he did on the luxury lines.

"It is lovely. And I am hoping that love of designing carries over to jewelry." He'd thought it up on a whim and then run with it. She liked designing clothes, so why not?

And it let her see him in action in the place he felt most comfortable.

The car slowed to a stop and he opened the door and reached for her hand. Her long legs slid out after him, the purple dress dropping to just below mid-thigh as she exited the car.

Damn.

Focus. That was what he needed. He'd brought her here for a reason. A special trip. Behind the scenes at the place where he gave so much of himself.

"The entry looks like any other office building entrance." Frankie hit her hip against his as they headed to the lifts.

"Did you expect it to look like a jewelry store?"

"Yeah. Kinda. I mean this is nice but it could be an accounting firm or legal offices." Frankie looked at the very standard office interior.

"Or a high-end matchmaking service?"

Andilet was boring inside. There was a reason one of Frankie's first moves had been to personalize the shoebox Amelia gave her.

"Touché." She stuck out her tongue as they stepped into the lift.

There was only one fun area of this place. The rest was for the admin work that took up far too much of Decker's life as CEO. Accounting floor one. Marketing on two. Public relations and legal on three. Office suites on four.

Dull. Dull. Dull.

But five. Floor five was heaven.

He slid his access card in the lift and punched in the code that granted access to the top floor.

"Now, that is different." Frankie raised a brow as the lift shot up. "Are you hiding valuables up here?"

"Of course." He pulled her to him, enjoying the surprise crossing her face far too much. "You thought the first floor would look like a jewelry store."

The doors slid open and he squeezed her before stepping out. "This is where the pieces come to life." He punched in a code and opened the security door for her.

"That is thick." Frankie swallowed and didn't move. "We aren't getting locked in, right?"

He didn't want to lie to her, but he could see the panic. "Yes. The door locks after we step through. But there is another keypad." He pointed to the right side inside the door. "So we punch in the same code and it lets us out. And if the building loses power, there is a backup generator good for six hours to make sure we can exit."

Frankie stepped through the door. "Backup generator for a locked room of jewels. Sounds like you got locked in once."

Decker couldn't stop the shudder as the door locked behind them. "Yes. Years ago, and not at Heughs. It was the first place I landed after uni and the owner was unimpressed by the design team's concerns when we were trapped for twelve hours. Told us that we should have used the time to produce."

"That is awful." Frankie's hands were on her hips. "How dare he!"

"If it makes any difference, that was the first company I took over, and I installed the same generator there that I have here. Not that I've ever needed it again." He shrugged. Security and generators were not what he'd brought her to see.

"Oh, cool. We had design desks like these at the design house. Though I liked using the tablet more. Give me a digital pencil and set me loose."

Noted. He preferred pencil and paper to start but if she wanted a digital pencil and tablet, not a problem.

"This is my area. I don't get to come in as often as I want anymore, but..." He unlocked his private studio and flipped the light out.

Frankie pushed up on him to look over his shoulder. Her breasts against him sent nearly all thoughts from his mind.

"Oh." Frankie squeezed past him. Her eyes wide.

There were all sorts of jewels along the wall. Not the best quality, but enough to give the temporary settings he designed life. Jewelry designs lined each wall, except for the one behind his desk.

With all the magnificence in the room, it was that wall drawing Frankie's attention.

"You do have a hobby." She crossed her arms and leaned against his desk. "Wow."

"They're just pencil drawings." He'd brought her here to show off the jewelry.

"So?" Frankie stood and walked over to one. One he probably should have taken down.

"This is me." She lifted her finger but didn't touch it. "The first day. The day you covered my shoes in coffee. I notice my feet aren't in it."

"I didn't notice your feet, sweetie." He'd drawn that after the meeting he'd been late for. She was all his brain wanted to focus on, and Decker had thought putting her on paper might drive Frankie from his mind.

A truly ridiculous notion now.

"What did you want to show me?" Frankie returned to his desk and hopped up to sit on the top.

He was never going to be able to work there again and not think of her.

"I thought you might like to try your hand at designing. It's not fashion, but the ideas are similar."

"Design? Like a ring, or a necklace? Oh, or a watch! You could put jewels in the face to make a garden. Florals haven't been big this season, but I think they'll be all the rage by next summer. You can see the trend starting to form in pockets of the influencing markets. Once they grab it for real, everyone will want it." Frankie snatched a piece of paper from his desk and quickly sketched the basics.

For someone who preferred a digital medium, she was more than adept with pencil and paper.

"How long did you work in the fashion industry?" Decker looked at the sketch, stunned at the quick thinking and focus on trends. Fashion moved faster than jewelry but trends still drove the industry.

"Not quite a year, but I loved fashion magazines growing up. I used to save up all my money for them, and when I got a phone, I devoured any haute couture I could find. I designed a few dresses for myself before my grandmother's ancient sewing machine finally gave up its creative soul. Probably good it's gone. No place for it in any of the flats I've lived in." She made a few more quick sketches.

"I don't know how you'd drop the jewels in, but that's your job." Frankie hopped off the desk, passing him the image.

It was perfect. A watch face designed in less than five minutes by a woman who'd never done it before. He could see the diamonds and rubies laid out in the flowers. Not too many, just enough to highlight the etchings in the face. This was the kind of piece professionals worked years to craft. And she'd done it without even thinking.

"You are a natural." A raw design talent. He'd met only one other, and he'd made sure to up Victor's salary any time the competition started trying to draw him away.

Frankie waved a hand at the drawing. "I doodled an idea. No big deal." She shrugged as she strode over to the jewels. "It's hardly an academic achievement to brag about. What's your favorite gemstone?"

No, she was not changing topics right now. He didn't know why her parents had fed her such a bloody lie. Designing was not something just anyone could do. "Just because your art isn't an academic achievement doesn't mean it isn't valuable. Do you know how much I pay my designers?"

"So—" she slid up to him "—if the dating coach thing fumbles, I can apply for a job here? Good to know. Now, *my* favorite gemstone is aquamarine. The blue ones, not pink. I mean pink is fine, but if you are going with pink, then pink sapphires make a better option. Or pink diamonds."

The CEO in him was screaming to grab a contract and offer her a sum no one could compete with. Pull her away from Andilet and give her all the design freedom she wanted. The man who wanted her, didn't want to taint this moment by offering her a job.

"Want to learn to set stones?"

"Will you have to guide my hands?"

The flirty smile drove all thoughts of contracts from his mind. "Absolutely."

Singing.

That was the only way to describe the fire dancing across Frankie's skin as they headed back to her place. He'd spent the evening showing her how to drop jewels into settings. Gripped her wrists as she used the jewelry pliers—even though they both knew she didn't need the support.

It was heaven and she didn't want the evening to end.

"Do you want to come up? I have some decaf tea." Frankie had no interest in tea, but she was very aware of the driver a few feet in front of them. The man hadn't turned around the entire time they'd been in the car, but she kept glancing at him. She bit her lip. "Or if you're ready to call it a night, then—"

Decker's lips brushed hers, silencing the offer of just saying good-night.

His breath was warm on her ear as he whispered, "I'm not sure I will ever be ready to call it a night, sweetie."

Sweetie.

He'd called Frankie that several times this evening. Usually she wasn't one for cutesy nicknames, but when an endearment rolled off Decker's lips, it made her toes curl.

The car parked and Frankie slid out after Decker, following him into the building.

"Looks like the lift is functioning again." Decker pressed the button and winked.

"Thank goodness." Frankie's cheeks heated as Decker ran his thumb along her wrist.

"That excited for tea?"

She could own up to what was driving her desire to get upstairs, but he was so sure of himself.

"Excited to be out of these shoes." She squeezed

his hand as she stepped into the lift and pushed the button for the seventh floor.

Time slowed when they kissed—that was enjoyable. Right now, anticipation was making the time it took to get to her flat drag horribly.

She forced herself not to race to the door, unlock it and pull him through.

She nearly dropped the keys as Decker's hands wrapped around her waist.

"You are so beautiful." He ran his thumb along her exposed stomach.

She turned her head, pressing her lips to his. It wasn't enough. "Are you trying to distract me?" At least she wasn't going to have to pretend to ask if he really wanted coffee or tea.

"Yes." He raised his hand just a bit, running a finger over her bare midriff.

The lock clicked open and they sighed in unison. She pushed the door open, threw her purse on the tiny bench she kept by the door for shopping bags and winter coats. Decker locked the door as she pressed herself against him.

"Frankie." His lips were on hers as she pulled him toward her bed.

The benefit of living in a tiny place was she was going to have him exactly where she wanted in no time.

"Frankie." Her name was like a prayer on his lips as he kissed his way down her neck.

As they got to the bed, Decker flipped their positions. Now it was Frankie sliding into the bed. He knelt, gently pulling her heels from her feet. "That is what you wanted most, right?"

Frankie grabbed his shirt, pulling her to him. "Maybe I just wanted you to worship me all night."

"Oh, we are definitely on the same page." He captured her lips as he slid between her legs. "This is the sexiest dress I've ever seen." He ran his fingers up her thigh as he feathered kisses along her mouth and neck.

His fingers trailed her upper thigh, never going quite high enough as his lips found each place that made her moan.

He was barely touching her. Not rushing the moment, but her body was a fireball. A bottled explosion.

Decker lifted and looked at the bow on her chest. "Is that just decoration or...?" One hand ran along the edge of the fabric while the other continued to caress her thigh.

"One way to find out." If this dress had gone to production, the bow would have been purely decorative, but as desire spun through Decker's gaze, Frankie was glad she'd never bothered to put a stitch there.

He suckled one breast, then the other as she stroked his length.

After a moment, he grabbed her hand and pinned it above her head. "As much as I enjoy those touches, I'm nearly out of my mind already.

And you are spinning me far too close to the precipice. I still have *so* many plans."

Frankie was nearly bursting herself. "Decker." She wasn't sure she could wait for all his plans.

Sliding her dress down her body, his grin widened. "You are the most beautiful woman I've ever seen."

Confidence in her looks was never something she'd lacked. Frankie knew she was conventionally attractive. Many men had told her she was pretty or gorgeous or beautiful. But the soft words falling from Decker's lips struck her differently.

Bending, he slid her dress and panties off together. Then he bent his head, his lips skimming kisses along her thighs, growing ever closer to her core. The touches were light, ghostly, and sent her soul spiraling. It wasn't enough and too much all at once.

Finally he licked her core and Frankie gripped her bedsheets as she crested. He didn't stop. Didn't change his motion, didn't adjust anything. And another wave crashed over her.

When he slipped a finger into her, Frankie let out a scream as he teased another orgasm from her. "Decker, this…is…amazing but I need you. All of you now." She slipped from his reach and grabbed a condom from her top drawer.

Her plan evaporated as she stared at him. "I'm naked."

His thumb stroked her nipple. "I noticed."

"And you—" she unbuttoned the top button of his shirt and pressed her lips to the bare skin she found "—are not."

Undoing the next button and the next, she followed the shirt's path with her mouth, enjoying every tiny hitch in his breath. When she got to his belt, she undid it, tossing it to the floor with his shirt.

Before she could undo the button of his pants, Decker's hands beat her to it. "Sweetie, I need you."

"That was all I was waiting to hear." She opened the condom and slid it down his length while her mouth worshipped his. Then they were joined. The symphony they'd created cresting to completion.

CHAPTER NINE

"YOU SMILE ANY bigger and I might just be sick."

Frankie looked up, shocked to see Amelia leaning against her doorway, the grin on her boss's face at odds with the introduction. "Not sure how you saw my smile with my head down."

"You are always smiling these days, Frankie." Amelia strode in and sat down.

Frankie looked at the clock—not quite fifteen minutes left in her day.

"I know what time it is, Frankie." Amelia shook her shoulders a little. "I wasn't always like this, you know. I used to be a good boss."

Frankie had no plans to pick up that verbal bait.

"The truth is we don't get clients like we used to. Yes, our books are full-ish." Amelia looked at her nails. "But we used to have a wait-list. Used to keep our matchmakers for years, now they rotate out every two years or so, if we're lucky."

She picked up one of the crochet owls Frankie had on her desk. Frankie had met with six clients this week, and each one had grabbed the owl. Maybe it was the size? She'd have to look and see if she had any others that size; if not she could whip one or two up.

Like with her clients, Frankie waited while Amelia rolled the owl around in her hand.

"I came in to apologize." Amelia let out a deep breath. "Several weeks too late." She gestured toward the shelf where Frankie had put a few self-help books. "Maybe I need to read one of those."

"You are welcome to borrow something. I like the last one on the left best, but a book won't help you fix yourself. They all say similar things. The best ones make you think about yourself." Frankie glanced at the clock again; how long was whatever this was going to go on?

"Another three clients signed up for the package that includes six dating coach meetings before they start the matchmaking process." Amelia sighed. "This little office might not be big enough if this continues."

"Are you upset that it's working?" Frankie had mixed feelings herself. The job was fine but the thought of doing it for years wasn't appealing.

She was trying to give it time. After all, dreams didn't always develop overnight.

"A little." Amelia let out a chuckle. "That sounds terrible but I met with marketing managers, paid an obscene amount of money to a private firm to get growth recommendations and not one of them came up with what is the most obvious side business for a matchmaking firm. No, that suggestion comes from the one client we couldn't find a partner for."

"Except you kinda did find him one." Frankie knew what frustration was like. She'd felt it in so many careers. Felt like a failure when she was technically doing everything just right.

This was Amelia's dream. Andilet was a London staple. It had been used by generations of high-class individuals looking for a partner. And she'd helmed the ship as it had started a decline.

That would send most people into a tailspin. But it had worked out for Frankie.

Amelia smiled, a genuine smile that made the corners of her eyes crinkle. "Yes, the one truly unethical thing I did worked out in a weird way." She stood. "The reason I came in here was to give you this." She laid a small envelope on the desk.

"What?"

"Your monthly bonus. Yours is calculated on the scale of coaching signups, and, if the last three weeks are any indication, I suspect the future ones will be quite a bit more lucrative." Amelia nodded. "I'm not sorry about how you started at Andilet. It started this, and you met Decker, but I am sorry that I was not more welcoming."

"Thank you, Amelia." Frankie stood, grabbing her purse. It was time to head out. She was a firm believer that a job only got the hours it paid her for.

Her wrist buzzed and she looked at the text scrolling through as Amelia headed out.

Life a little hectic. Meet at my place for dinner instead of going out?

Sure, but I need the address.

Frankie bit her lip as she waited for the address to come through. Decker had slept at her flat nearly every night for the last two weeks. They'd go out, then head back to her place.

She was excited to see where he lived. And terrified.

After all, there was no way Decker Hughes lived in a seventh-floor studio apartment. No way he walked up tons of stairs when the lift broke...often.

The address came across and Frankie took a breath before typing, Be there soon.

Stepping into the early evening, she started for the tube, but as she got closer an idea broke forth. He was running behind; it would be fine if she took a quick detour. Decker might not even notice.

Less than an hour later she stood outside one of the fanciest high rises in London.

Probably the fanciest.

You knew he was a multi-millionaire, Frankie. Hell, maybe even a billionaire. What did you expect?

"Ma'am? Can I help you?" The doorman tilted his head as he looked her over, his hand on the walkie-talkie at his hip. Like he'd need to call backup?

"I'm meeting my—" Her voice died away. Her

what? They'd hung out for almost a month, but the first two weeks of that hardly counted.

"Who are you meeting?"

"Decker Heughs?" She hadn't meant to make it sound like a question but she could tell from the man's response that he heard the uncertainty.

"What is his passcode?"

"Passcode?"

"Move along, ma'am. Don't make me call security." The man crossed his arms. A woman walked past him, nodding and taking a long glance at Frankie.

Frankie wasn't going to skulk away. She was an invited guest. One who didn't know the passcode, but that was easily rectified.

Pulling out her phone, she called Decker, putting the phone on speaker. "You didn't give me your passcode."

"What passcode?"

Now it was the doorman squirming. Interesting…

"Yeah?" She turned her gaze on the burly man by the door. "What passcode?"

"Sorry, please go in." The man opened the door, his eyes on the floor.

"What is your name?" Decker barked the command, and the man's face paled.

"No need for that. A lesson learned. See you in a minute, Decker." Frankie smiled at the doorman. "Lesson learned, right?"

His shoulders loosened. "First day on the job and I saw you scoping out the place. They said people have been trying to get in to see—" The doorman clammed up abruptly.

"I see. Trying to see somebody wildly famous who deserves their privacy." She nodded. "I'm Frankie. Hope the rest of your first day is smooth."

"Nice to meet you, Frankie."

She strode into the building and had to force her feet to keep moving toward the lifts. This place screamed luxury in an understated tone. There was nothing gold, nothing too flashy.

But the seats in the corner were upscale leather, the floor a freshly polished high-end wood and the green lights of security cameras green blinked in every corner. Her building had cameras, but she'd heard from more than one reliable source that they were "for show."

In other words, broken and not on the repair list.

She pressed the lift buttons and stepped in. This place was a reminder that Decker had fulfilled, and surpassed his career goal. And she... Well, she was moving forward with something that had career potential. If she could convince herself to settle for *good enough*.

Decker had ordered takeout and put it in the oven to keep warm. He paced the expansive kitchen waiting for Frankie to arrive. He'd nearly headed down to the door when she'd called.

Passcode. He'd never required such a thing. There were several celebrities in the building but he'd put Frankie's name on the visitor list the day she took him mudlarking.

The decision had been more a hopeful prayer to the universe when it had seemed he might lose her. All the doorman had to do was ask her name and the party she was visiting.

This was one of the reasons he liked her place so much. It was relaxed. Tiny, but relaxed.

Her place was a home. The penthouse was sterile.

He opened the door and smiled as the lift doors at the end of the hall opened. Frankie stepped out, carrying one shopping bag awkwardly under one arm and another in the opposite hand.

"Give me that." He took the bag from her arm, shocked at the light weight. "Why are you carrying it that way? It's so light."

"Art pads." She kissed him, then held up the other bag. "And pencils. Don't want to bend the pad."

"I have pencils, Frankie." He led her to his door and swallowed as she stepped into his flat.

Frankie froze at the entry. ".Whoa."

His place was giant. He'd briefly dated one woman who swore she was with him for the flat alone. A funny joke...until he realized she wasn't kidding.

"It's large."

"Oh." Frankie nodded. "Sure, it's a penthouse, but this." She walked to the window that looked out over London. "How do you leave? You must have one of the best views in the city."

Stepping next to her, he put an arm around her waist. "The view is certainly nice now." His focus was solely on her. He'd never paid much attention to the view. He was rarely here. In the last few weeks he'd stayed at Frankie's and before that he'd spent far too many nights sleeping in the office.

Frankie didn't turn away from the window. "You never even notice it, do you?"

How did this woman see directly into him?

"No." He turned his focus to the view. It was gorgeous. "I hired an estate agent to handle the deal. She found it, got me to sign the papers and even found the furnishings."

"That why it's so sterile?"

"I was just thinking that before you got up here. Your place has character."

"My place is jam-packed because it could fit into your living room at least twice." Frankie finally turned in his arms and captured his mouth.

He drank her in. Today's meetings had taken so much out of him. And nothing bad had happened. It was simply draining to be kept in meetings all day when he could be designing.

When she broke away, she walked to the bags she'd brought. "I'm not hungry yet, you?"

"Not really." He looked at the bags. "Why the drawing material?"

"It's a game I saw on social media. And since you're such an apt artist, I figured it would be fun to give it a go."

"I'm not really." He sketched things out but unless it was jewelry he struggled to make it look real. Except for the picture of Frankie. That was the first time his hand had drawn exactly what was in his memory.

"Yes, you are. You have a hobby; you just use it to make money instead of having any fun with it." She pulled the two drawing pads out of the bag, handed him one, then tossed the fresh pencils at him.

"No 5H pencil?"

"Not an artist, you say?" Frankie laughed as she headed to the large kitchen table that he'd never used. "That is a beginner set. A 5H is not a beginner pencil."

"Should be. It helps with shading." Decker stuck his tongue out and started to sit next to her.

"Nope, you have to sit down there." She pointed to the other end of the table. "That is the game. Trust me."

"Fine, but we are eating dinner in the living room on the couch, together. Not like some ancient royal family at the heads of the table." He gathered his supplies and gave her a wink.

"Now that you're done with your fit," Frankie giggled, "we are drawing each other."

"What?"

"I saw several cute videos. Technically they were all painting each other, but paints are much more expensive and harder to store." She held up her pencil. "You have twenty minutes, go!"

"Twenty minutes?" Her hands were already flying across the page as he opened the drawing pad and looked over the pencil selection. There was no way he could do Frankie justice in twenty minutes. It was nearly criminal.

"Twenty minutes." Frankie didn't look up from her pad. "That is the game. If you have all day, then you will tweak it endlessly."

That was true.

"Why was your day so long?"

Frankie's question hit him as he sketched the first line. "I had meetings all day. No time in the design room."

"Mmm."

"No other comment?" He wasn't sure why he expected more commentary on the statement. No one liked going to meetings. There were memes and online forums dedicated to joking about three-hour meetings that should be three-line emails.

"Meetings are my life. I met with two new clients today and six more signed up. You are the only one that got dating coach experience in the wild." Frankie laughed. "And look where that landed us."

Decker liked where it had landed them. "They're missing out, but I will admit that I'm a little miffed no one else will have to go mudlarking."

"Hey! You said your mother and stepfather love to do it."

"I said my stepfather likes it and my mother loves my stepfather."

The timer on Frankie's phone buzzed and Decker frowned. He'd barely started.

She turned her page around and his mouth fell open as he stared at the caricature. His head was massive and he was sitting on a little artist stool bent over the tiniest artist desk ever.

"I worked at a fair for a brief bit," Frankie explained. "You can make decent money from the tourists with these."

"Is there anything you haven't done?" The woman had tried so many things. Excelled at them. Now she was starting up a new focus in an established firm.

"Stuck around." Her tongue darted out in jest. "Let me see yours."

Her words were so loose, so hurtful toward herself. Before he could say anything, his front door opened.

"Decker!"

He shot to his feet as his mother's scared call echoed into the flat. He grabbed his phone, dialed his stepfather and tossed the phone to Frankie. "Let him know my mother is here. I'm sure he's terrified."

Frankie didn't ask any questions. She just grabbed the phone and he heard her calm tones explaining what he'd said to Harry over the line.

"Mom, how are you?" She'd never wandered, though their doctor had told them it was a part of the disease that would come. And after that came the locked facility and... But Decker wasn't thinking of that now.

"Was I coming here?" His mother twisted her hands together as she looked around his penthouse flat. "Were you expecting me? Tell the truth."

Decker bit his lip as he weighed his response. She seemed clear right now. And lying was something the dementia physicians recommended against. Redirect. That was the goal. That stemmed the frustration and anger that boiled to close to the surface when the disease took hold.

"I wasn't expecting you, but I am so glad you are here. I have takeout keeping warm in the oven. Curry from the Indian place you like so much."

"Curry." His mother tapped her finger against her lip. "I think Harry was planning to take me to dinner. I..." Her eyes filled with tears. "I was with him, then I wasn't, and nothing looked familiar even though I used to live in this damn city."

There was the anger.

"You found your way to me." *Thank goodness.* "Harry says he isn't far and should be here shortly. Would you like some water?" Frankie was there, glass in hand as she smiled at his mother. A serene look on her face as she held the glass out. "It's warm out."

"It is warm." His mother took the glass, lifting it with two hands. That had been one of the first symptoms. Instead of holding her coffee or water in one hand like she'd done all her life, she'd held it like a toddler.

Without even noticing.

After draining the glass, she passed it back to Frankie who disappeared and returned with another. They repeated the process twice more.

"Wow." His mother blinked and moved to the sofa. "I am feeling a lot better."

"Dehydration," Frankie murmured in his ear as she moved to his side.

"Yes. Dehydration." His mother tapped her head. "Memory is spotty on the best days but the hearing, that I have in spades."

She looked at Decker. He ran inventory over her frame. Was she thinner than last month? Maybe a hair. Was she lucid? Right now, yes. Well-kept? At the moment.

"Since my son has lost his manners, I'm Nina, Decker's mother."

Frankie held out her hand. "Frankie."

His mother raised a brow. "I gave a title with my name. You got one, or is my son holding off on labeling your relationship?"

The glare she shot Decker brought a smile to his face. It wasn't the intended effect, but he was so glad to see his mother as herself. The clarity, the sharp tongue. The smile.

"Frankie is my girlfriend, Mom." Decker put his arm around her. She didn't stiffen at his words. Didn't immediately correct him. But she wasn't leaning into him, either. This was hardly the best way to make such an announcement, but the beam on his mother's face was worth it.

"Girlfriend." His mom clapped her hands. "A girlfriend." She put her hands in her lap, probably registering the awkwardness. The dementia was robbing her of emotional control.

Just little bits here and there. She was trying so hard to keep it under control.

"So how did you two meet?"

"I was a fake date set up by the matchmaking agency he hired three years ago. He was a notoriously hard to match customer, so they sent me undercover to figure out what made him tick. I got in a little too deep, and the next thing you know." Frankie kissed Decker's cheek before strolling over to the oversized chair. "Here I am."

There were words sputtering across Decker's brain but not a single one found its way to his lips. That was the honest answer, but *hell*.

"Notoriously hard. Because he doesn't do anything but work? Not a single hobby, or anything that makes him fun. You sure you want him to call you his girlfriend?"

Somehow he'd lost complete control of this conversation.

"Oh, but he does do fun things. We just drew pictures of each other, without the other looking, as a game. He can draw so well. I'll show you." Frankie popped up off the sofa and headed toward the kitchen.

"Frankie." Decker didn't want to leave his mother, but that picture was a nude.

CHAPTER TEN

GIRLFRIEND. GIRLFRIEND. GIRLFRIEND.

Maybe if Frankie managed to figure out where Decker kept the pods for his coffee machine, her brain might have enough caffeine to focus on something other than his announcement to his mother and then stepfather, who arrived five minutes after she'd realized the image Decker had drawn was a nude.

It had hardly been the only admission last night. After Harry had taken Nina home, Decker informed Frankie he'd joined the dating agency because of his mother's illness. That he'd wanted her to see him happy.

And that he felt like he was letting her down.

After that realization he'd shut down. Which she understood. Dementia was a tough diagnosis. Her grandmother had suffered from it. The disease robbed you of the person years before they left this world.

But he'd made his father's dream come true. What if saying *girlfriend* was simply his way of making that dream happen in a moment when it was possible?

She wanted to be Decker's girlfriend. But she wanted the title to be more than a goal reached for another.

Ugh. There was no caffeine in her bloodstream and these thoughts were far too deep for a decaffeinated brain.

Frankie bent, rummaging through the bottom cabinet. Seriously, did the man actually use his kitchen? The layout made no sense.

Of course he doesn't use it.

Frankie let out a sigh as the realization popped in. In pursuit of his father's dreams, Decker worked and worked and worked. He ate out, at the office or ordered takeout. His fridge had some eggs, butter, cheese, milk and spinach—that she'd tossed because it was wilted beyond repair.

Did he not even have coffee?

"Coming into the kitchen and finding you bent over in just my T-shirt is the best way to start the morning."

Frankie was tempted to shake her ass, and if she'd had coffee, that might have been an option. Sex was a good way to put off what might be a tough conversation—not a healthy choice but...

"Where is the coffee, Decker?" Frankie didn't attempt to stifle her yawn as she stood and showed him the empty mug. "I need caffeine."

"The first time I saw you, you had coffee in your

hand." He walked to the cabinet over the fridge and dug two pods out from the back.

That was not where anyone who drank coffee regularly at home kept their goods. "You have your assistant put your coffee on your desk right before you arrive, don't you?"

The color creeping up his neck and the sheepish grin as he handed her the pod was more than enough confirmation.

"If I had a fancy machine like this..." Frankie pulled the mug from the base of the machine and took the first glorious sip.

"You would still have coffee waiting for you at your desk." Decker's lips brushed her neck as he reached around her and put his pod and mug in.

His free hand slipped under the shirt she'd worn to bed last night, a finger trailing from her belly button to the top of her panties. "You in my shirt..." His lips trailed along her neck down her shoulder.

"You didn't finish that sentence." She leaned back.

"Didn't need to."

Frankie enjoyed the shift in his focus from her neck to her mouth.

The coffee dinged, but unlike her, he didn't reach for the mug right away.

"Your coffee is going to get cold."

Decker took her coffee, ignoring her pout as he lifted her on the counter. He pulled his shirt over her head, then placed the coffee back in her hands.

He stepped back but rather than reaching for her, or his coffee cup, he darted out of the kitchen.

"Hey!"

"Don't move. Except to drink your coffee." The last bit seemed like an add-on.

But she took advantage of the free moment to enjoy another blast of caffeine.

When he came back in, he had a sketch pad. Not the one he'd used yesterday. This was not a beginner pad. And the pencils he'd grabbed certainly included the 5H he'd missed last night.

He grabbed his coffee and leaned against the other side of the counter, his head bent for a second, then focused back on her.

"You already have one nude of me." She'd nearly brought it out to his mom. Luckily, when she'd sheepishly walked in with hot cheeks, Harry had just arrived and the conversation had shifted.

"That was a quick sketch and I didn't have time to finish your face."

Frankie let out a chuckle. "My breasts were fully crafted."

Decker took a few steps forward. The end of the pencil ran along the base of one nipple, then the other. Each hardened under the soft touch.

And the man isn't even directly touching me.

He made a few changes on the pad, then ran a finger, one lonely finger, along her belly, hovering just above her panty line.

Her breath caught. When was he going to set the pad down?

Before she could ask, he stepped back and returned to the page. She took another sip of her coffee to bury the question.

Tension boiled in the quiet as she nursed her coffee and he sketched on the pad. Every few minutes he stepped up and touched her. With the pencil, with a finger. Never with his mouth.

Fire danced across her body with each caress. But it wasn't enough.

"Decker." She swallowed the moan creeping its way up her throat as his bright eyes caught hers.

"Frankie." He smirked, clearly aware of how turned on she was.

"How long until your picture is done?" She wanted him. Wanted to strip the clothes from his body and make sure he was as enthralled as she was.

"I doubt it will be done for a few weeks. You may need to sit for me a few more times."

His gaze sparkled as she set her cup down. He was in front of her, the pad and pencil left behind, in milliseconds.

"You're the one who wanted coffee before anything else," he said. Kisses were feathered along her breasts as his fingers trailed up her thigh. "Did you get your caffeine fix?"

He moved her panties to the side, his thumb pressing exactly where she'd wanted him for what felt like hours. She ran her hands through his hair as her body quaked from its first release.

"Mmm…" He slipped a finger in, his body holding her in place when all she wanted was to slide from this counter and straddle him. "Yes, this is the best way to start the day. You should sit like this every morning."

He stroked her, his mouth and hands worshipping her as she lost the ability to think of anything but ecstasy, need and him.

It wasn't until she was on the tube home that Frankie accepted the reality that they'd let their bodies do the talking this morning. Which meant they'd never discussed the announcement he'd made so freely to his mother.

Decker's mind was not on the weekly staff meeting happening around him. It was nothing compared to tweaking the beauty on his page that was Frankie.

After she'd left this morning, he'd run a finger over the sketch, reliving the moment. He'd stood in that kitchen hundreds of times. Poured coffee. Grabbed a snack, when he remembered to hit the shops on his way home.

Or ask his assistant to do it.

He rarely took advantage, but today he'd asked Miranda to stock the kitchen and buy more coffee pods that he could set right by the machine. Because he'd not been kidding when he told Frankie that he wanted her to sit for him several more times.

"Mr. Heughs, do you have any thoughts?" The voice was pointed. Not angry, but only because Decker was the CEO.

"My apologies, Dillan." The marketing manager was standing at the head of the table, outlining something Decker had clearly missed. "I fear my mind got lost. I apologize, again, but can you please repeat?"

Dillan's shoulders moved but he didn't let out the sigh Decker knew was in the back of his throat. Fair enough.

"I was saying that we need something fresh on the marketing floor. Our jewelry is fantastic, of course."

Of course.

It was Decker's designs on the cover, but Dillan was right. They'd not drastically changed up the images in a year.

Their highest priced items sold largely based on quality and exclusivity. Decker's contacts in the celebrity market added much to his bottom line. But there was a place for marketing.

Many marketers might enjoy being in a slower paced business with a steady clientele, but Dillan was craving more. Decker expected he'd see his resignation before long, but until then he deserved his boss's focus when he was presenting.

"How about a watch campaign?" The suggestion from Kinsey, the Chief Financial Officer, got several head nods. "I mean, we focus on the jewelry but there is a huge market for upscale watches."

"And you would know." Steven, the head of human resources, pointedly looked at the piece on Kinsey's wrist. "Pretty sure that isn't one of our pieces."

"Maybe if there were more options, it might be." Kinsey held up her watch as Decker stood.

"Give me one sec."

Just before the door closed, he heard Dillan let out that sigh. "Where is his head today?"

"Focused on his new girlfriend." Kinsey gave a friendly laugh. "Finally found someone that makes him lose focus."

Lose focus. No. This was just one meeting.

He was still digesting Kinsey's words when he walked back in with Frankie's floral watch design. "Would you wear something like this, Kinsey? The stones could be upgraded or downgraded depending on the price point the customer is looking for."

"Oh, my gosh. Decker, when were you planning on showing us this? A floral design. With rubies in the flower or just the center of the daisies with yellow gold diamonds." Kinsey ran her hand along the edge of the design paper. The watch-collecting CFO clearly saw the exact same thing Decker had seen.

A perfect design.

"Did you or Victor craft this? Because it needs

to be in production now." She passed the design over to Dillan.

The marketing manager nodded. "A few more floral faces would be good. Give us some variety in the program."

"You or Victor, Decker?" Kinsey smiled. "'Cause I need to know where to shower my praises.

"Neither, actually." Decker clicked his tongue as he met the CFO's gaze. "Frankie designed it. On a whim when I was showing her my studio."

"On a whim." Kinsey took the paper back from Dillan. "Your girlf—" She caught herself. "The woman you've—"

"My girlfriend, Kinsey. The one you all think is making me lose my focus." His CFO opened her mouth, but Decker rushed on before she could say anything. "Frankie designed that. And yes, on a whim."

"So are we offering her a consulting fee or putting her on the payroll?" Kinsey pulled out her notepad as the company attorney, David, who rarely spoke in these meetings, did the same.

"Not the payroll. She has a job."

"Not one paying her close to what we pay Victor, I bet." Kinsey didn't stutter but she didn't push, either. "Any chance she'd design a whole line for us? I'll run the numbers, but I figure the design fee on the line, with the expectation for growth," she looked at Dillan who nodded, "seventy-five thousand pounds. With a bonus of twenty-five thousand for every unit over a hundred sold?"

"I can ask."

The room nodded, certain that Frankie wouldn't be willing to turn down the offer. Decker was fairly sure she'd say yes, too.

That was a good thing. But if she was designing here, it would be even harder to put her out of his head when he needed to focus on the day-to-day operations.

He could manage. He wasn't his father. Frankie was lovely and he enjoyed time with her more than anything, but that didn't mean he was losing focus.

Decker typed out a quick note that he had something to discuss with her and asked her to meet him at the flat.

She texted back quickly agreeing to come by as soon as she was done for the day. Then asked if he'd be there by then.

Of course.

He looked at his calendar, then stared at the text. Maybe he shouldn't have sent it so quickly. No, he could push that meeting he had later to next week. No issue.

This conversation was company business, anyway. Yes, he was planning to find a way to keep Frankie at his place all weekend, maybe in his shirt and nothing else...

Decker cleared his throat. If he was going to meet her on time, he had to focus.

* * *

Frankie hadn't thought much of Decker's text, until the doorman of his building had to let her into the penthouse.

"Mr. Heughs's meeting ran late. He'll be here soon." The man gave her a soft smile. One she was trying very hard not to read into.

That was almost an hour ago. She looked at her phone and the unread text she'd sent off thirty minutes ago. All right, there was no need for her to hang out at his place indefinitely. She'd played this game with the last guy she thought about getting serious with. He'd set something up and then get tied up at work or forget or something.

Frankie had set him free. She wasn't ready to do that with Decker, but she was not going to hover in his penthouse, hoping he'd show up when he'd asked her to come.

Grabbing her purse, she headed out the door. Closing it, she hesitated for a moment. No, the doorman had opened the door; he could lock it back up just as easily.

She headed for the lift, forcing her head up. She wasn't going to let whatever this was sidetrack her.

He left you at the ghost hunt.

That was weeks ago. It was before the girlfriend label. Things happened.

We've never discussed the label.

Her brain was in overdrive. The thoughts weren't helping her sour mood.

The doors opened and the doorman was standing there holding a bag.

"Mr. Heughs sent along dinner and a note." The man passed the bag over, then looked at the door she'd closed. "Do you want me to lock up?"

Frankie looked at the bag. Her belly rumbled as her nose caught the scent of spices. Vietnamese. One of her favorites.

"No. I'm hungry. If he isn't here by the time dinner is in my belly, then I will take you up on the offer. Sorry you've had to run his errands."

"Part of the job." The man tipped his head and let the lift door shut.

It was well past when the chicken pho Decker had ordered her was gone when Frankie finally heard the door of the flat open.

"I have a good excuse."

Excuse. She'd have preferred he led with an apology. Running late was one thing, but avoiding her texts, that was a whole other thing.

"I don't want an excuse." Frankie was already miffed at herself for sticking around this long. If it were any other guy, she'd have left long before the food showed up. And she wouldn't be picking up anymore phone calls or texts.

But here she was.

Decker paused. "It's a really good excuse. Trust me, you're going to like this one."

Frankie stood, grabbing her purse. "I don't care about the excuse." If he didn't recognize the need for an apology, then this wasn't a real relationship. And her heart couldn't get more invested.

Decker set his bag down and walked over to her, "I am sorry. I really am. I was in a meeting, hashing things out on a contract. I left my phone on my desk and—" He took a deep breath. "No excuse. I should have called or at least texted."

"At least."

"But…" He pulled a stack of papers out of his bag. "It is worth it. It took longer than expected for legal to draw up the contract, I wanted to make sure that you were fairly represented if…"

Decker's voice trailed off.

Legal. Fairly represented. Why would she need representation? "Decker, speak clearly please, why are you holding a stack of papers?"

"They are your contract."

"No." Frankie shook her head as the penthouse started to spin. She'd heard wealthy clients discuss the nondisclosures they wanted with potential partners. The contracts for how things were to go. She had no interest in paper defining her relationship.

"I am your girlfriend, or at least that's what you told your mother. I am not signing some girlfriend contract. If that's what you want, then—" The words *we're over* wouldn't come. But it was true. She was not signing some relationship contract drawn up by his office legal staff.

The papers fell to the floor as Decker moved toward her. But she stepped back.

"Frankie, it's not that. Man, I have screwed this up royally. It is a contract for design work at Heughs. A limited contract for watches."

"Watches?" Her ears were buzzing. "What the hell are you talking about?"

"We needed a new marketing strategy. I was in a very long meeting this morning. Made longer by me replaying our kitchen escapades instead of listening. But my CFO is a huge fan of watches, and she loves your design." He held his hands out but Frankie didn't move.

"My design?" She crossed her arms, to keep herself from stepping into his arms until she fully understood.

"The watch face, with the florals, which will be all the rage next season? The watch face you designed in minutes to the envy of this—" he pointed to himself "—designer who would have spent weeks doing it."

The watch face he'd been so fascinated with weeks ago. The one he'd complimented like it was something superspecial. "It was just a watch face with flowers."

"It was not." Decker frowned and walked back to the contract and picked it up. Then he stepped back and threw it on the coffee table. "And that is the proof of it."

"Meaning?" She looked at the document, well aware that it could say just about anything. She'd worked in a lot of roles, but not a single one in the legal field.

"Heughs Jewelry wants your design, for seventy-five thousand pounds. Well, that design and two more. The marketing guys like threes. They sell well."

Seventy-five thousand pounds. For three drawings. "What's the catch?" She'd taken far too many jobs in her life not to understand the line if it sounds too good to be true…it probably is.

"No catch. Really. The team wants watches. They want something fresh. I showed off your design. Contract." He passed her a pen.

A pen. A contract. His smiling face.

Seventy-five thousand pounds.

"See, good news. Worth being late for, right?"

The pen was heavy in her hand. This was a good thing. Something that would make life easier. So why was there a lump in her stomach?

"If you ever want to quit Andilet…"

"I like my job." Mostly. Sure, it didn't have the creative side she'd enjoyed so much in fashion. But it was hers. "I'm not leaving it."

"I know." Decker kissed her head, but there was something in his expression. A hope that she'd change her mind?

Or maybe excitement for her.

"I'll design the watches, and sign this, but from now on, even if it is a contract about me, I need a heads-up on schedules."

"Absolutely." Decker brushed his lips against hers and then watched as she signed her signature.

It was only as she was lying awake later that she realized she hadn't read it, hadn't even questioned it. And once more they'd gone to bed without discussing their relationship.

CHAPTER ELEVEN

"WELCOME HOME, GORGEOUS." Decker grinned as he heard Frankie walk into his flat. For the last three weeks this had been their routine. One of them got to his place and started dinner.

She wasn't technically living here, but her makeup and a few changes of clothes were here. Though she wore one of his shirts to bed every night. That was a tradition he had no interest in changing.

"I look like a mess." Frankie rounded the corner of the kitchen and dropped her stuff on the bench right outside it. "And I feel even worse. I dropped a client today because..." She gestured to herself.

"What the hell?" Her dress was covered in brown stains. He pushed a few buttons on the oven to make sure dinner stayed warm.

"Soda. It's soda." Frankie's lip trembled, but she didn't let any tears fall. "I pointed out to a client that perhaps marrying to make their grandparents happy and ensure their grandmother didn't cut his inheritance was not the best way to start a union."

"And he threw his drink at you?" His body

was vibrating but this moment wasn't about him. "Who?"

"I'm not telling you. Even if I was cleared to." She looked at her dress. "I don't think this is salvageable." Now the tears did fall. "I made this one. I sketched it out and searched for months for the perfect fabric. I made it on a rented machine and now…" He reached for her and she stepped back. "I'm sticky and gross."

"Okay." Decker pulled her into his arms and held her while the sobs racked her body.

"This is so dumb. It's a dress. An outfit. It's nothing that important. No great achievement. No—"

Decker laid a finger over her lips. If he ever got to meet her family, he was going to have more than a few things to say about the fact that they had trained their daughter to look at all her gifts and see them as worthless.

"Nope. It is an achievement." He ran his hand up her back, soothing motions. "You designed it. Searched for the perfect fabric and then crafted it with your hands."

"Anyone could do it."

"They absolutely could not." Decker had been furious with the cretin who'd tossed his soda on her. Fury did not come close to the emotion racking his body at Frankie's utter disregard for her achievement. This was a big deal. And even if it wasn't, she was allowed to have feelings about it.

"Let's shower, get you into something comfortable. Then I have pasta made and a surprise." He'd been working on something for the last week, or rather he'd hired a few people to work on it while he and Frankie were out of the flat.

Decker had planned a big fanfare but that wasn't what she needed right now.

"Not sure I feel up for getting busy in the shower, Decker." She pressed her lips to his. "Not that having you naked is ever a bad thing."

That hadn't even been a consideration when he'd mentioned it. Frankie had had a rough day and he was caring for her. Period.

"This isn't about that." Decker pulled her toward the giant walk-in shower. He started the shower, then turned to her.

Unzipping the dress, he wondered if there was a way to get the stains out. He knew nothing about fabric. But maybe. Though if Frankie said it was ruined, it probably wasn't salvageable.

"I love this bathroom. I know that is such a ridiculous thing to say, but the shower is perfection and I don't have to duck my head to get the water in my hair." Frankie laughed as she took off her bra and slipped out of her panties.

Decker stripped and led her to the shower. "This was the reason I bought the flat. This room. So I don't find it ridiculous at all." He turned so Frankie was the one standing under the hot water.

Grabbing the soap and a washcloth, he gently washed her body.

"Who would have thought working at a matchmaking firm would ruin outfits?" Frankie let out a laugh that didn't have a ton of humor in it as he turned to her to clean her back.

"Outfits?" Decker grabbed the bottle of shampoo he'd purchased after seeing it in her bathroom. He ran his fingers through her hair, massaging her scalp.

"Hmm. That feels so good."

"Good. It's supposed to. Now, outfits? Did someone else toss something on you?" One person was bad enough, two or more…

"Coffee. On my shoes." Now her laughter was real. "Though I guess that one worked out okay since I'm naked in the shower with him." She turned to rinse out her hair.

"I have it on pretty good authority that you hated those shoes and it was an accident." Decker let her finish rinsing, then turned her back around to add the conditioner, making sure to pull the condition all the way to the tips of her curly hair.

"Should I be concerned that you're so good at washing a woman's hair?" Her soapy body was pressed against his as she rested her head on his shoulder.

"It's not that hard to figure out." He pressed his lips to her forehead. "You had a long day, pampering is the least I can do." She'd needed this, and he needed her.

Needed.

Loved.

The words wrapped through his brain. He needed her. Because he loved her. He loved Frankie. Decker wasn't sure when that had happened. But there was no denying it.

Why would I want to deny it?

Because it's terrifying?

What if you screw it up and lose her?

He didn't need his brain to provide such unsolicited commentary.

"You said there was a surprise, too." She pulled back and started to rinse out her hair.

"I do have a surprise. A good one. A perfect one."

"Perfect." Her breasts lifted as she let out a sigh and smiled. "That is a pretty high bar to reach."

"It is. But you're worth it."

The smile vanished as she shut off the water. "I don't know about that, but I do know that I'm very excited to see what it is."

Frankie stepped out of the shower, grabbed a towel from the warmer and headed into the bedroom.

And Decker stood, towel wrapped around his waist and wondered what it was going to take to get the woman he loved to understand just how special she was.

* * *

Frankie pulled her wet hair into the bonnet she kept at Decker's place and looked at herself in the mirror. How had she gotten so comfortable so quickly? She flew from relationships almost as fast as she turned in her resignations.

But somehow this felt right.

"Surprise time?" Decker stuck his head in the bathroom and raised both his eyebrows at the same time. He looked like a little kid, excited for some treat they were showing their parents.

Frankie had been that kid once, at least according to her parents. They'd joked about how as a child she was always showing off her drawings. It had not been said in an approving manner. Not a cute, fun family memory.

And not one she shared. If she'd ever done it, she'd picked up fast that it wasn't wanted.

"You're very excited about this." She laughed as Decker grabbed her hand. "I hope I live up to the expectation."

"You always do."

That wasn't true but Frankie wasn't tarnishing this memory like her parents had done.

Decker walked her across the penthouse suite and went to a room that she'd not entered. "What is this?"

"The surprise." Decker let out a little huff. "Obviously."

Frankie tapped his shoulder. "A room is not a surprise, Decker."

"This one is. Close your eyes."

Frankie closed them and heard the door open.

"No peeking," Decker chided as he led her into the room.

"I am not peeking."

"But you want to."

That was true. She stuck her tongue out, but didn't open her eyes. This was important to him. So it mattered to her.

"One...two...three...open."

Frankie followed the command and all the air left her lungs. A sewing machine was in one corner, a mannequin standing beside it. A serger sat not too far away on its own table. An ironing board, with the iron, hung on a wall. There was a table in the center of the room cutting fabric and a design table, with a tablet and digital pencils.

Decker walked over to one of the floor-to-ceiling cabinets on the back wall and opened it to show space for fabric and notions. "I wanted to stock it, but honestly, I am not sure which fabric is which. Jewels—" he kissed his fingers and gestured with his hand "—those I know like the back of my hand. But when I asked Miranda to find someone who knew the best way to set up a sewing room for a fashion designer, the person she contacted recommended letting you choose. Which of course makes sense." Decker bit his lip. "Are you going to say anything?"

Her lip was trembling. Tears were coating her vision. He'd made a space for her. A space for just her.

"If you're worried about the yarn." He walked to another cabinet and opened it to show a bunch of yarn, and some hooks. "These were Mom's. She has a ton still, but she isn't using them as much these days."

Decker's voice caught and he crossed his arms as his gaze focused on Frankie. She needed to say something. Needed to force words of thanks out. No one had ever done something like this.

"Decker." Her voice trembled as she looked at the room that was bigger than her entire flat. "I don't know what to say. I don't, it's too much. It's perfect and it is too much and I… Thank you."

"So you like it? It's the right stuff? I admit that I know the design table, we use those, umm, but the rest…" He hesitated. "You can tell me, if I got something wrong."

"No. I mean it. It's perfect. It's as though you pulled one of the sewing blog pages off the internet and added everything a designer dreams of." Frankie spun slowly, taking it all in. "I used to tell my grandma that one day I'd have a sewing room. And we'd make everything we wanted. She always patted my hand and told me to dream big." Frankie swallowed the lump in her throat.

She hadn't been with Decker that long, but he'd created something. For her. Seen a need, a want and just made it happen. Frankie looked at him, and her heart exploded.

She was in his arms without knowing how she traveled across the room. His grip tightened on her waist and he held her while sobs racked her body.

"I'm sorry." She let out a hiccup. "I really love it."

She'd been drawn to him since the day he spilled coffee on her yellow shoes. Craved him on their first fake date. Done her best to keep her distance and fallen headfirst, anyway.

She loved him.

Love.

That wasn't an emotion she'd allowed herself to feel in any of her previous relationships. Though if she were honest, none of them would have made even a tiny effort toward making this dream a reality. They hadn't even heard her dreams of designing.

But Decker had heard the cry from her soul and healed a wound she hadn't acknowledged in so long. "Thank you. Thank you so much. I can't wait to bring things to life in here."

"You're very welcome." Decker's lips pressed to her forehead as her stomach let out a giant rumble.

"Right now, though—" he grabbed her hand "—it is time for dinner. No arguing. You are famished and my stomach is gurgling in agreement."

He led them out of the room, chuckling as

Frankie looked back at it for a minute. "I promise, you have all the time in the world to play in there later."

All the time in the world.

That was what she wanted…with him. What a wonderful and terrifying thought.

CHAPTER TWELVE

"Wow. Look at this place" Decker leaned against the door of the sewing room. Every night in the two weeks since he'd led Frankie here, he'd come back to the flat to find her in there. Tonight she was at the drafting table, but there were fabric swatches on the cutting table and photos of women in floral dresses on the wall.

She'd made a dress like the one the jerk had thrown soda on. Not quite the same and she discussed its imperfections rather than celebrating that she'd mimicked nearly perfectly the one that had been ruined. The woman only saw flaws. It drove him nuts.

"Yeah, I guess you could say I've made it my own." Frankie leaned on the drafting table, her dark gaze turning to him. "Doesn't mean that I haven't noticed you staying later and later at the office." She looked at her watch and sighed. "Did you eat there or are you famished?"

"I grabbed something at the office." Decker's neck heated. He'd lost complete track of time—again. It was a habit he was trying to break, but after years of reaching out and getting him at all hours, it was hard for clients and staff not to have access to him constantly.

Frankie nodded but he could see the disappointment in her eyes. He hadn't meant to stay at the office so long, but the mock-ups for next season's winter line were in. Including Frankie's watch faces, which would go perfectly on the wrists of the women she'd put on the wall.

"I made a few more of these." She handed him two more watch faces, a group of earrings and three rings. "Any interest?"

"Yes." He was already thinking about which jewels might work best in the rings. There were a few clients that liked an overly busy ring, but most preferred subtlety. And these rings were designed to go either way. It was such a skill—one she barely recognized.

"These are great, Frankie. Do you have thoughts on the jewels?" He had some but he wanted to hear hers.

"Yes. I think you should do these as spring colors. Pinks, purples and greens. The others are in the winter collection, so these are about revival."

"And then we do a summer and fall collection." Decker was already envisioning the shift from pinks and purples to brighter jewels. Things that would show the vibrancy of summer and then the shift into autumn with oranges and chocolate diamonds.

"Yes. I could do those, too." Frankie smiled but it didn't quite reach her eyes.

"We'll need to do another contract. Maybe put you on a quarterly contract. Or you could come to work for Heughs full-time. I promise no one throws sodas on you, talks down to you or spends the entire session talking about how to get their exes back." He started toward the living room. The light was best in there and he wanted to send a few pictures of these to the board. He was betting that Kinsey would call first dibs on the second watch face in this set. She'd bought one today off just the mock-ups and these two were even better.

"Decker?"

He heard Frankie call his name down the hall, but he wanted to get these sent off. Wanted her to see how quickly her designs were celebrated. He snapped the pictures and forwarded them.

"Decker." Frankie was beside him and he jumped.

"You snuck up on me." He leaned in to kiss her, but she pulled back.

"I didn't sneak up. I walked up but you were so focused on the silly drawings that—"

"They aren't silly. Do you know what the expected earnings are from the initial three watches you designed?"

"No and I don't care." Frankie held up a hand. "I wanted to discuss the Andilet clients whose bad behavior you threw in my face."

"I didn't throw them in your face. I just mentioned the downside." Decker hadn't meant anything by the words. But soda guy was seared into his brain for what he'd done, how low he'd made Frankie feel, though she refused to give him any identifiers. And the other two were complaints he'd heard over dinner last week.

"Two days ago, you complained that this season's earrings were not selling like anticipated. That your head designer was vacillating between furious that no one could see the genius in the designs and questioning whether he'd lost all of his abilities to function as an artist." Frankie took a deep breath, then continued, "And yesterday you were complaining about sitting through another marketing meeting. But—" she held up a hand to forestall him "—last week you also gushed about the clients who found the perfect engagement ring and the artist who plans to wear a piece you selected when she receives her lifetime achievement award."

Decker waited a second but she seemed to have run out of steam. "I am sorry. I didn't mean to throw them in your face."

"That isn't the point of my tirade, Decker." Frankie sank into the oversized chair, curling up into herself. No way for him to slide in and hold her.

Probably the point.

Decker was missing something. That was clear but he wasn't sure what.

She bit her lip and shook her head. "What good things have happened this week in my job?"

"What good things?"

Frankie laid her head against her knees. "The woman, whose whole problem was her parents telling her she wasn't good enough, going out on her first date with a man who was genuinely interested in her. The man, who hated the fact that he is supposed to marry even though he has no interest, agreeing to go to counseling to get support for telling his family about his asexuality."

"I hear you. And I do remember those things." Sort of. He had a vague memory of her discussing them. But they weren't as front and center as the negative examples.

"Do you?" Frankie gestured to the pictures on the table. "Or are you only hearing things that might help you get me to leave Andilet and go work for your company?"

He grinned. "I would love for you to design for us. I mean—" he gestured to the table just like she had "—you are so good at it."

"Decker."

"I can't say I am joking, Frankie. I know jewelry design isn't the same as the fashion world. But it is a close sister and you are a natural."

"So natural I got fired." Frankie rolled her eyes.

"I am growing a new part of Andilet. I am helping people. I am enjoying what I do."

Her voice faltered just a little on that last bit. Because she was angry with him or because she was trying to convince herself it was true?

"Do you realize the longest conversation we've had all week was about the seasonal jewelry?"

He opened his mouth, then closed it. It wasn't. It couldn't be. But he swallowed as he racked his brain, trying to think of anything more substantive since the night he'd taken care of her after the soda incident. How had two weeks passed so swiftly with so little discussion?

"I'm sorry." There was nothing else for him to say. "I really am, Frankie. I get excited about jewelry and the work and running the company. I was—" He caught the final words. He'd doubled down at the office because he'd heard the board talking about how she distracted him.

And in the process made her feel alone.

Damn it.

"It's okay."

"No, Frankie. It's not." He sat on the edge of the oversized chair, not crowding her, but being present. "I heard the board say you distracted me and—"

"I distract you?" She uncurled a little and he took the opportunity to slide in next to her.

"You do." He kissed her cheek. "In the best way possible."

His phone buzzed and she raised a brow. "Do you need to get that?"

"I am sure it is just Kinsey squealing at the idea of a season of watches. The woman owns at least twenty watches. She's a true collector—and your biggest fan."

"Oh, please." Frankie kissed his cheek and started to get up, but he grabbed her by the waist and pulled her into his lap.

Then he took his phone out and smiled as he saw Kinsey's text. "Told you so."

He held up his phone showing her the words.

These are the best. I want one of everything. Tell Frankie she is a genius!

"Genius?" Frankie took the phone out of his hands.

"Yes. Genius." Decker kissed the top of her head. "You are a raw design talent. I've run into exactly one other one."

"Who?" Frankie tossed the phone into his lap.

"My head designer." Decker nodded to the designs on the table. "You have a gift, Frankie. I am not arguing for you to leave Andilet. I *am* arguing that you need to recognize your talents are something others crave."

"*And* you need to focus on balancing work and home life." Frankie pushed his shoulder. "I don't want to keep eating dinner alone."

"Fair." That was an easy enough ask. He could balance things better. He could.

Frankie rolled her eyes as soon as her latest client walked out of the room. Today was their third meeting and the man was not ready for dating. Period.

She sent an email to Amelia. Her boss was not going to like that Frankie was recommending another client be placed on the *Do Not Pair with a Partner* list. Technically this was only the third client they'd completely cut loose. There were many who'd signed up at the firm for the dating coach advice, who were lovely people.

Those who were ready but tired of the dating apps. Tired of the same small conversations. Ready to expand their dating game and find their person. And so far two of the original clients were already in serious relationships.

A few others were hitting it off with some of the people they'd been paired with.

But two—now three—were dangerous. *In her opinion.*

Setting them up with a partner would be negligent at best. But that meant losing revenue in the short term.

Frankie hit Send on the email, then grabbed her purse. She didn't have any clients this afternoon and she was not spending any more time in this office. Walking past Patricia, she smiled at the little turtle on her desk. Frankie had worried her colleagues might think her crochet animal gifts were silly, but they all loved them.

Even Amelia.

"If the boss asks, I am taking the afternoon off. The last client—"

"Is a manipulative creep that has more than one partner who alleged abuse only to get quiet very fast, usually after a cash windfall." Patricia let out a shudder. "It's in the gossip pages. Amelia doesn't read them, finds them slanderous."

Frankie looked at the closed door, barely controlling her own shudder. "I personally agree with Amelia on the gossip pages, but there is something wrong with that man. I have my cell, if anyone needs me."

No one was going to need her. But at least she'd offered.

Her job was fine but she wasn't hunting up new clients. Wasn't upselling each new person that sat in the chair across from her. Much to Amelia's disdain. They either wanted dating coaching or they didn't. Frankie wasn't a pushy salesman.

The sun was shining as she walked into the Heughs Jewelry headquarters. The security guard waved as she walked to the lift and punched in Decker's code. If she was cutting loose this afternoon, then maybe she could convince him to do the same.

As Frankie stepped out of the lift, she ran into

a short woman, whose eyes instantly looked like they were going to pop out of her head. "You're Frankie."

"I am. Sorry, I don't know you. At least I don't think."

"Oh, sorry. Kinsey Mathews." She held up her wrist. "Watch enthusiast. And the winter mock-up for your floral faces…" She let out a little squeal, then looked around to make sure no one was around.

"Just us." Frankie winked.

"Good. Chase in accounting can go on and on about football. Complaining and cheering, depending on how the game goes. Mark talks cricket like it's a religion and if I hear any more about gambling on horse races from Nigel…" Kinsey shook her head. "But God forbid I mention my watches!"

"It does seem like woman's interests get comments that men never have to deal with." Frankie's sister had stopped talking about her love of fan fiction when her high school boyfriend told her she sounded dumb.

Frankie had tried to encourage Catalina. Told her that the stories she read and wrote were fun. But Catalina had buried her head in her studies even more. No fun. Nothing. The women in their family were academic successes.

Until me.

"Well, I am glad you like my little designs."

Frankie started for Decker's office but Kinsey's hand gripped Frankie's wrist.

"They aren't little designs. I know we offered you a contract for the season's selections but if you wanted to work in any jewelry house, they'd hire you on the spot with those in your portfolio."

"I am pretty sure Decker would flip if I set out to work for one of Heughs's competitors.

"He would, indeed." Decker rounded the corner and shook his head. "Not sure what I've walked in on, but yes, that might miff me." He winked and looked at Kinsey. "I see you finally met Frankie."

"Yes." Kinsey squeezed Frankie's wrist one more time, then dropped the connection. "She is amazing, just like you said." Kinsey raised a hand toward Decker and headed down the hallway without any more comment.

"To what do I owe this surprise at three in the afternoon?" Decker pulled Frankie into his arms and dropped a light kiss on her lips.

It wasn't enough but they were in his office hallway.

"I've come to convince you to play hooky with me." She pressed her lips to his, holding them for a second longer than was professional. "Come on, Decker."

He was wavering, but this morning when she'd said she would basically be running from one appointment to another until lunchtime, he'd bragged that his day was going to be light on meetings. And pointed out that all Frankie's meetings took place in her office—no running necessary.

He looked at his watch.

"You said you didn't have meetings today." Frankie pushed her lip out, overaccentuating the pout. "Was that a lie?"

"No." Decker pressed his lips together. "No, it wasn't." He swallowed. This was clearly seriously difficult for him. "All right, where are we off to?" He held his arm out.

She linked them immediately, pushing the button to call the lift. No way was she giving him time to think longer about this.

"How about we go window-shopping while the shops are open? Then we can grab a meat pie or something before heading ho—" She caught the word. Decker's flat was his still. She stayed there nearly every night. Or rather every night. But it wasn't *home*.

Neither is my flat.

"We can watch movies and basically lay around for the evening." It would be a fun walk, plus she wanted to see if that small heart-shaped stone she'd seen in that oddities shop's window was still there. Her office had a perfect place for it. And then relaxing all night in his arms would drive away the tense feelings her client had left in her belly.

"Of course." Decker took a deep breath as the doors of the lift closed.

"You sure?" Despite her intentions just ten seconds ago, if he wanted to stay, she wouldn't cause a fuss. This was spontaneous—something that wasn't Decker's specialty.

He looked at her as the lift headed down, "Honestly, no. I've never played hooky. I know that is probably *shocking*." The tapping of his foot as he made the joke gave away how uncomfortable "sneaking" away made him.

"It is not." Frankie leaned up and kissed his cheek. "But once in a while, on slow days, it's freeing." Decker needed time away from the office, and she needed time with him.

"Then let's go window-shopping." Decker laughed and waved to the security guard as they headed out the door.

Decker chuckled as Frankie made a face on the way up the lift to his flat. Home. She'd nearly called it home at his office. The flat had never felt like home to him. Not really.

It was a place. A status symbol his father had never received. A point to show Decker had reached the pinnacle he'd driven himself to.

But with Frankie there. With her sewing room and the multicolored blanket she'd crocheted lying across the top of the white couch, her makeup in the bathroom and the oat milk she craved for her coffee in the fridge, it was home.

"Did you have fun on your first day playing

hooky?" Frankie kissed his cheek as they stepped out of the lift.

"Yes." It wasn't a lie, either. He'd enjoyed himself and hadn't thought of the office after they stepped onto the London streets. His phone had been on silent as he walked with Frankie through the shops.

"Did you have a good time?"

"It was just what I needed." Frankie let out a sigh. "My last client was a manipulative ass who we've blacklisted from the company."

"Blacklisted?" Decker dropped the fruits and veggies they'd picked up from the shop on the way home. "I wasn't aware Andilet blacklisted clients."

"They don't. Or they didn't until the dating coach service started. Which is wild." Frankie pulled her shoes off her feet and then took her bra off. It was a ritual she performed every night before walking into the bedroom and getting into comfortable clothes. "But now that everyone sees me for at least one session before paying and signing up to the matchmaking service, we can see who might not be ready."

He followed her into the bedroom.

"I think you really hit Amelia when you brought up the broken relationships after joining the firm. At its heart Andilet is not that much different from your company."

He didn't agree with that assessment, but he was

too busy enjoying the image of Frankie undressing to press the issue.

"She has to change for the company to survive. Change is hard, even when you want it. When you don't?" Frankie slid a pink cotton dress on and dropped onto the bed with him. "Thank you for coming today. It was fun, even if what I was looking for was gone." She kissed his lips, then darted off the bed. "I'll make the popcorn… You pick out a comedy for us to watch."

He selected a recent rom-com she'd discussed and took the popcorn bowl as she sat next to him on the couch. "What were you looking for?"

"Huh?" Frankie's gaze met his as she popped a few pieces of popcorn into her mouth. Damn, her lips were so lush.

"I thought we were just window-shopping and getting fresh air." Decker took a few pieces of popcorn, too. He hadn't realized there was an agenda for the day. But if there was something she wanted, he might be able to find it elsewhere.

"Oh, it's nothing." Frankie waved her hand and picked up the remote.

He took it before she could press Play. "What was it?" The woman had a tendency to push any wants away. She would listen to clients, even difficult ones, and help them figure out what they wanted in a partner. But when it came to something she wanted, Frankie tended to wipe it away as no big deal.

Her needs were just as important as others.

"A little pink stone in the shape of a heart. I saw it in the window on our first date. It was small and no big deal, I mentioned how I thought it would shine in the right light. I have a spot in the office where I was going to place it. Decker?"

He was already across the room when she called his name. He knew exactly which stone she was discussing. And knew for a fact that it did sparkle in the sunlight. He grabbed the box and headed back for the couch.

He sat back down and handed it to her.

"Wait—" Frankie looked at the box in her hand and then at him. "No. You didn't."

"Open the box, Frankie." He'd bought it the day after their date. He'd called the store the second they opened and had it delivered that night and planned to give it to her when she had a bad day or just needed a happy thing.

Frankie looked at him. "Why?"

She still hadn't unwrapped it. "What do you mean, why?"

Frankie shrugged. "I mean, I didn't do anything. Didn't earn…" A tear fell on the pretty wrapping paper as she stared at the box.

Clearly she'd never gotten something without having to earn it. The night he showed her the sewing room, she'd mentioned living up to his expectations, and now that Decker thought about it, she was using it nearly every night. And had designed more watch faces at the desk.

Was she using the room for pleasure or to "earn" it?

"Hey." Decker lifted her chin, hating the tears slipping down her cheek. "You don't have to earn anything here."

Her lips pressed against his and her arms were around his neck as the box fell, still unopened, into their laps.

"I love you." The whispered words were barely audible as she broke away from him.

"I love you, too, Frankie." Three little words. He'd planned a grand celebration to accompany them. Well, he technically hadn't planned it yet, but he'd expected to lay on more fanfare. A nice dinner out. A moonlit walk.

Yet, here, tonight, on the couch in lounge pants with a bowl of popcorn ready for devouring was somehow so much more perfect.

Frankie smiled as he brushed the final tear from her cheek. He picked up the box and held it out. "Want to open your present now?"

CHAPTER THIRTEEN

DECKER DROPPED A kiss on Frankie's head as he slipped out of the bed. She let out a little groan but didn't wake. She'd be in the kitchen the second the aroma of coffee hit this room.

He grinned as he looked back at the bed one more time. The woman was curled into his pillow, her bonnet protecting her curly hair. She looked so peaceful.

And she loves me.

After their declarations, they'd settled into the sofa and watched the movie. It was so normal. Perfect in the simplicity.

His phone buzzed as he headed for the kitchen. He wasn't quite the must-have-coffee-before-anything-else person that Frankie was, but he functioned better with a little caffeine in his system.

Decker pulled out his phone as he started his pod.

Leona Pierce stopped by yesterday for you. I told her you were out. She was not happy and will be stopping by sometime today. Just a heads-up.

Miranda didn't add any additional details. No doubt the staff had taken some verbal abuse from the matriarch who still believed an ancient family title meant they were somehow above everyone else. And that their loan granted them perpetual access to him.

Why didn't you call me?

Decker scrolled through his texts and missed calls. Nothing from Miranda. Nothing.

She and her husband came at six thirty. You'd been gone for hours; the rest of the staff was gone, too. Just giving you a heads-up for today. Not like she is easy to please on good days.

Six thirty. If he hadn't cut out of the office early, he'd have been there. Just. He'd made a pact not to stay past six thirty since Frankie pointed out the hours slipping by him.

He could have made an exception. Just once.

"Is that your coffee or mine?" Frankie yawned, stretching her arms above her head, revealing her belly button. "Any interest in drinking it in bed? We can snuggle—"

"No." Decker blinked as the words flew from his mouth. "Sorry. I just. I have a client I need to see. They came by yesterday and I'd snuck away."

Frankie bit her lip as she moved to grab her own mug.

"I'm sorry," he said.

"You already said that." Frankie took the mug from his machine, handed it to him and then started her own coffee.

He had already said sorry. The Pierce account was the most important account by volume alone. His father had lost his business by losing the most important accounts over time. The losses made him weak, made the company vulnerable to acquisition by rivals.

Decker's gaze floated to Frankie. He wasn't his father. Frankie was important to him. He loved her. Yesterday was perfection.

At least until this morning.

"So you're staying late tonight." It wasn't a question.

Maybe that should bother him, but all he felt was relief. She understood. "Yes. I need to rectify this for the client."

"Did you forget an appointment?" Frankie leaned against the counter, the mug in her hands, her dark gaze rooting him to the floor.

"No. But these clients are used to having access to me whenever they want. They are the ones I had to satisfy the night I left the ghost hunt."

Frankie flinched, then straightened her shoulders. "Why didn't Miranda call while we were out? Or text? You could have been back at Heughs's HQ in no more than twenty minutes from every place we were at."

Decker shook his head as he downed his coffee. "These clients don't wait twenty minutes. And they came at six thirty when everyone was headed out."

"Then they should not have expected services." Frankie's matter-of-fact statement made sense in the real world. But the world of the excessively rich was not the real world. They were accustomed to having any whim fulfilled.

"Work at Andilet for much longer and you'll see that certain clients' expectations are very different than others."

Frankie shifted her shoulders and set her mug down. "I will be working at Andilet for the foreseeable future."

"I know."

"Do you?" Frankie crossed her arms. "Because that statement sure sounds like you are hoping I hang it up."

Decker held up his hands. "Clearly we both need more coffee because this is not the way to start any morning. Particularly after we said *I love you* for the first time last night."

He stepped toward her, his hand nearly on her waist when his phone buzzed on the other counter. He hesitated and Frankie looked down. "Go. But no client is worth staying late for. They are people."

"With limitless pocketbooks." Decker read the text. Leona Pierce was going to be at Heughs the moment the headquarters opened. Which meant he needed to leave thirty minutes ago.

"Still people."

"I need to get going. I am going to dress as quickly as possible and I will see you tonight." He blew her a kiss. "Love you."

"Love you, too."

Not the best way to start the day, but he'd make it up to her.

Frankie spun the pasta around her plate and listened to the book club podcast that usually put a smile on her face. She'd hoped that listening to the podcast on her headphones might trick her brain into thinking she wasn't alone, but that illusion had ended long before the first episode. And she was onto her fourth.

She didn't bother to look at the time. It was well past dinnertime. She'd waited, then finally made herself a plate—not that she was eating any of it. The futile hope that Decker might walk in and join her still clawing at her heart.

He ate at the office.

She didn't technically know. But at the same time, she did.

They'd had a perfect day. He loved her. She loved him. And then this morning he'd panicked over a meeting that hadn't even been scheduled. Difficult clients were part of life. Hell, you were always going to have someone that thought because they paid a bill, you owed them all your time.

Boundaries.

Decker needed boundaries and to find a way to think of his business as a business instead of an extension of himself. If the business had a bad quarter, which was going to happen at some point no matter what he did. Limitless growth wasn't an option in business. There were always down years. When that happened, he needed to know it wasn't a reflection on him. The worst part was that Heughs was at the top of its game and Decker still wasn't enjoying the success.

Her phone buzzed and Frankie smiled as she tapped the Bluetooth earbuds. "Tell me you are on your way home?" She hoped that had sounded like a question…or maybe she didn't. It was past time for Decker to have crossed the threshold.

"I mean, I *am* home, but since when do you care about my schedule?" Her sister's voice echoed in the earpiece.

Frankie looked at the pasta and stood. There was no point in trying to eat anymore.

"I thought you were someone else, Catalina. What can I do for you?"

"No 'how are you'?" Catalina let out a little huff on the other side of the phone.

"Were you planning on asking how I am doing?" Frankie wasn't usually this direct with her family but she was too tired to play games.

"I know how Flyaway Frankie is. Happy. Content. Floating through the world like nothing matters."

Frankie opened her mouth to correct her sister, then closed it. Catalina could tell her what she called for or not.

After a moment her sister took a deep breath. "Sorry. I didn't really mean that. I just. You're always so happy. The family sunshine who can change with the wind and keep a smile on her face."

"Doesn't mean it's easy." Frankie pursed her lips as that truth fell forward. She and Catalina weren't close. They'd been set up as competitors their entire lives.

And Catalina always won.

"You hide it well." Catalina sucked in a breath. "I didn't get the promotion."

"You just got a promotion a few months ago. How many promotions are you planning on racking up this year?"

"None, apparently. I was told the job was mine, I've even been working as the head surgeon for the unit for the last four months and today…" Her sister sucked in a breath. "Today they let me know they'd decided to go with an outsider. A fresh voice."

"I'm sorry." Frankie meant it. It sucked to not get what you deserved.

"Yeah, well, temporary setback. But that's why I'm calling you."

"Because I know how to deal with career setbacks?" Had her sister finally realized that Frankie's last job was the career she'd truly wanted?

Her gaze floated toward the back room. The design table. The jewelry. That was fun. As fun as designing clothes.

More fun than being a dating coach.

Frankie pushed that away. Flyaway Frankie was not leaving her job at Andilet. Not giving up her place. She was staying.

"No. Because you're a matchmaker."

Frankie made a sound into the phone. An unintentional gasp. "What?"

Her sister was cooking, or slamming something metal together in the background. Keep busy when disappointed. That was something they had in common.

"You *are* still a matchmaker, right?"

"Not technically." Frankie headed to the design room. If she was going to listen to whatever this was, she wanted to be doing something with her hands. Doodling, crocheting, something.

"Already given it up?"

"Promoted." Frankie bit the word out. Technically not 100 percent true. But not untrue, either. She had her own office, met with more clients, got bonuses for retention.

"Oh. Why didn't you tell us?"

No *congratulations.* No *way to go.* No *how did you manage that in less than four months with such an impressive company?*

Because her family expected success. Demanded it. Nothing else was rewarded.

"Why do you want matchmaking services, Catalina?" Frankie took out a piece of paper and started the doodle. A circle with tiny teardrops etched into it.

"I need a husband."

This was why Frankie was doodling. Because the pencil in her hand, the ring taking shape under fingers had enough of her focus to keep the four-letter word buried in her throat.

"I take it the surgeon hired has a family." Frankie was impressed that her voice was so calm. Maybe working with the demanding clients at Andilet made this easier.

Catalina blew out a breath and Frankie could practically hear her sister rolling her eyes. "Yes. And they actually hinted that was the reason he was selected. Can't technically say it 'cause it would be illegal. But he has a wife and kids and as a pediatric surgeon, why don't I? I am probably looking for it and will have maternity leave and that will inconvenience the department."

"They said that?" That couldn't be legal.

"Of course they didn't say *that*." More pots banged together in the background. "But it is the words said between the lines. The innuendos on my dating life. The looks. All women see them."

That was unfortunately too true. The world expected women to play the role of mother, housekeeper, career-woman, wife and saint. All with no complaints or expectations of more from society.

"That isn't a good reason to start a family."

"Please. There is no good reason to start a family." Catalina huffed. "Mom and Dad love each other, but we were afterthoughts at best."

Your achievements got you attention. And my failures earned the wrong sort of attention.

That was such a bitter thought it brought tears to Frankie's eyes.

"Catalina, have you considered that maybe it isn't a terrible thing to miss out on the promotion? I know you wanted it. But you have worked and done nothing else since—"

"I am not a quitter, Frankie. You don't care and can flit from thing to thing. Not me. If you won't help me, fine." The call ended.

No goodbye. No time for Frankie to explain she was worried that Catalina would look around one day and have nothing but work. No friends. No hobbies. Nothing to look forward to besides the office.

Like Decker.

She swallowed as she looked at the time on her phone. Nine thirty. She bit her lip, pulled up his number and weighed the option of calling or texting. She didn't want to be a nag but this wasn't acceptable, either.

The front door opened and Frankie let out a sigh. He was home.

"Frankie! Frankie!"

"In the sewing room." She stood but he was at

the door before she could even move away from the drafting table.

"Oh, were you working on something?" Decker moved around her, the kiss he aimed for her cheek missing as he looked at the ring she'd sketched.

"Not really. Catalina called, upset, and I doodle when I—"

"Not really, Frankie?" Decker looked at the ring with teardrops etched into its side. "This is perfect." He snapped a picture, typing out a few things on his phone.

"Decker, it's late and I already ate."

"Me, too. Grabbed something at the office. Mrs. Pierce didn't show until seven. Can you believe that?" He walked past her.

She was tempted to stay exactly where she was, but Frankie didn't want to be petty. "Yes, I can believe that."

He'd dashed out of here this morning because Mrs. Pierce had indicated she was already on her way. But rather than show when she'd said, she'd taken all day. To prove a point, that her time was worth more than anyone else's. A point Decker had reinforced by staying to wait.

He pulled a bottle of wine out of the fridge, poured a glass, which he handed to her, and then poured one for himself. "A toast!"

"To?" Frankie didn't lift her glass.

Decker looked at her still-sitting glass. "Your success. This." He held up the doodle.

"That—" Frankie pointed to the ring "—is something I did while talking to my sister about a promotion she lost out on due to being single. I drew it as she called me untalented, uncaring for my career or myself, then hung up on me. *That* belongs in the trash."

Decker shook his head, "No, sweetie. It belongs on the finger of Leona Pierce who is going to pay a ridiculous sum of money for a Francesca original." Decker grabbed her glass, put it in her hands and clinked them together.

"Francesca original?" He'd never called her by her full name. In fact, he was the one who'd told her how ridiculous it was that Amelia wanted it changed.

What was that even supposed to mean? She'd explained the horrible things her sister had said and he was still holding up his glass of wine. Still acting like tonight was a great night. One for the history books.

"Stop with the celebration and explain or I am going home." She set her glass down and headed for the door. She hadn't slept in her apartment for almost a month, in fact most of her stuff had found its way here, but Frankie was too emotionally exhausted from dealing with Catalina, and waiting on Decker, to wonder why a simple doodle was making him so excited.

Decker followed her, the glass still in his hand

but as he got to the threshold, he blinked. His smile faded as he finally took her in. "Frankie?"

The tears that she'd kept in while talking to Catalina hovered in her eyes. "Are you explaining or not?" Her eyes cut to the wineglass and he looked away as it registered that it was still in his hand.

"What happened?"

"I told you what happened." She pulled her purse across her body, another barrier between them.

Decker looked back, like the words he clearly hadn't heard would materialize behind him.

"I wasn't listening. I am sorry. I was just…" His words died away and he cleared his throat. "Leona Pierce and her entourage arrived at seven. I think they thought that I would have left."

"You should have." Frankie didn't care about the heat in her words. She was here. Alone. No text. No I'm-running-late call. Nothing. And then he'd marched in on her upset and he hadn't even registered her pain. Hadn't listened to the words, just looked at a dumb drawing and gotten far too excited.

"This is *my* company." He pushed a hand through his hair. "I know I stayed late, and I am sorry. But these clients are very important. They purchase a lot of jewelry and they wear it places most people will never see the insides of because of their wealth."

"So you need to keep them because of their purse

size and access to clients too snooty to wear what the average Englishman or woman wears. Got it."

Decker frowned and shook his head. "It's not exactly like that."

"But close enough." This conversation was exhausting. "What does it have to do with me?"

"They love the seasonal designs you did." Decker held up the doodled ring. "But they want an original. A piece no one else will have access to and they want it to be the first Francesca piece Heughs ever produces."

Frankie bit her lip. "Let me guess, marketing says it sounds better if you use my full name, right?"

She didn't give him time to answer. No point to it, anyway. The answer was clear on his features.

"I'm spending the night at my place. Good night, Decker."

CHAPTER FOURTEEN

FRANKIE WAS RUNNING LATE. She'd arrived late yesterday, too. Hopefully not looking just as worn as she felt. There was no pep in her step. No excitement. Just plain old Frankie.

Something about not sleeping next to Decker was messing with her internal clock. And the tears staining her pillow weren't helping, either.

She should probably forego the coffee. But the pot in the office was so bland. No sugar. No artificial sweeteners. No fancy syrups.

Amelia swore the clients preferred it that way. Frankie suspected it was another cost-cutting measure.

Either way, she knew as the tube doors opened that she was heading for the coffee shop. What would five minutes matter in the grand scheme?

After all, there were no client meetings until the afternoon. This morning was eaten up completely by an all-hands meeting. One of Frankie's least favorite corporate-world things.

But a necessity. And she was technically considered a team lead. Of course her team only had one person—her. But she planned to pitch an event at the end of her slide deck.

A garden party. For the staff and clients. A get-to-know-you event. This way they could see how the clients interacted with each other in a laid-back setting. But also with staff and waitresses. Frankie had worked in the service industry and you could tell a whole lot by the way people treated those they thought were less than themselves.

Plus the firm could see if there were any sparks between clients they didn't expect. Currently Andilet's proprietary matchmaking "algorithm" seemed mostly to involve matching people up by class and one or two common interests.

Most of the clients were happy enough with the partnerships that created, but Frankie wondered if that was more because of Andilet's reputation. Find a partner in less than three months or your money back—and Andilet had a "100 percent success rate."

Many people struggled going against the expectation. No one wanted to think they were the reason to break such a "historic" streak.

Her presentation didn't state that outright. But it was certainly an undertone throughout it.

Decker was unusual in his ability to push past the expectations.

Decker.

Her brain wandered to happy memories and the

empty feeling rolling through her soul. Today was a busy day. She had plans.

Didn't change how much she missed him.

She moved up the station steps as fast as her feet would carry her. If there were a way to run from memories and sadness, Frankie would spend her last coin to have it. Unfortunately she was stuck with the longing ache in her chest.

"Frankie!"

Decker's voice was rough as it reached her ears. *Maybe he's sleeping as poorly as I am.*

He'd asked her to come home last night. Asked her to let him make her dinner and apologize but she'd made an excuse, not ready to make nice. His offer had seemed pretty appealing in this morning's light.

And her refusal felt petty when she looked at the empty pillow next to her.

Turning, she couldn't contain the smile brought on by the sight of him. And the two cups of coffee in his hands.

"You're late, so I'll be fast." He passed her the coffee and waited a second while she took her first sip.

The man knew her well.

"I am so sorry, Frankie. I was so focused on the business and the client that I just…" Decker kicked the ground. "I just couldn't see what I had in front of me. Come home. Please."

"You'll be home for dinner?" Frankie looked at

the coffee. There was more to say. More to discuss but she was late and she didn't want to. She wanted to go back to the penthouse. Wanted to sleep next to him and put this behind them.

"Absolutely." Decker started to lean toward her, then caught himself. "Can I kiss you?"

Frankie lifted on her toes and brushed her lips against his.

"Get a room!"

She giggled against his lips. "Seems like we've heard that before." Maybe it was a good omen.

"Seems like it." He kissed her again and stepped back. "I'll see you tonight."

"All right." Frankie squeezed his hand. "But a coffee won't end every argument."

"But it is a good start, right?" Decker winked. "As long as it's not on your shoes."

Frankie shook her head and waved as they headed in the opposite direction. Taking a sip of her coffee, she relaxed for the first time in several days. They'd had a spat. A big one, but relationships took effort.

"You look peppy." Patricia raised her eyebrows. "A little less gloomy now?"

"That obvious, was it?" Frankie had felt sullen but she'd always prided herself on covering her emotions. Hell, her family thought she had no feelings at all, apparently.

"Yes." Patricia didn't even bother to sugarcoat it. "But I am happy to see your smile. Not sure how long you will hold on to it, though, because quarterly meeting time." The receptionist made a mock fanfare gesture as she stood up from her desk. "The worst part of quarterly meetings is they happen quarterly. Ugh."

"Don't let Amelia hear you make that noise." Frankie raised her coffee. "And…" She pulled a few crocheted animals out of her bag but held them back from her friend as Patricia reached for them. "You have to listen to my presentation and answer questions to get these." She dumped them back into her bag.

"Bribing the audience—it just might work. Brilliant idea."

As they headed into the conference room, Frankie wished it were a brilliant idea. Instead the animals were the result of insomnia and misery. When her hands were busy and her mind focused on counting stitches, she wasn't thinking about Decker. Or at least it wasn't the only thing her brain was focused on.

The misery was over now. She was headed to his place for dinner. New day.

But we've had a new day before.

Frankie bit her lip as she sat down in the comfortable office chair. Andilet had splurged for upscale chairs in this room because it was where clients signed their contracts.

And now I am thinking of chairs instead of the issues between us.

"Frankie, why don't you start?" Amelia's tone was upbeat. She was clearly the only one truly excited for this quarterly meeting.

But if Frankie was presenting, then her brain wasn't allowed to wander to anything other than what she had to discuss. She was a team lead. Of a growth area. And she was going to rock this meeting.

Frankie was on her way. She'd texted about thirty minutes ago to let Decker know that the tube was delayed. He'd offered to have a driver come pick her up but she'd pointed out that by the time the driver arrived and she sat in London traffic, it would be easier to just wait it out.

She'd also said she had big news and was nearly busting at the seams to share it. He had news, too. He was a little worried about sharing it, given that it had caused their argument. Still, Mrs. Pierce had loved the piece Frankie referred to as a doodle. It was so much more than that.

If only she could see the full worth of her work.

Her family had damaged her belief in herself. Looked at her achievements and thrown them away because they weren't associated with their definition of success. Like there was only one way to reach the pinnacle.

He heard the door open, and Frankie called his name. "Decker!"

"Frankie!" He laughed as he echoed her call.

She rounded the corner, beaming. "We had our quarterly meeting today."

"I think you might be the only person I've ever seen start a conversation about a quarterly meeting with such a huge smile." Decker sighed as she stepped into his open arms.

He ran his thumb along her lower back, caressing her, relishing the fact that she was here.

Two days was two days more than he ever wanted to spend without her again.

"I know. I was not looking forward to it. And honestly I paid attention but there was nothing groundbreaking after my presentation." She leaned back, her cheeks darkening. "I know that sounds like I am so full of myself, but I promise it was really good."

He didn't doubt it. Frankie wasn't university-trained, but she'd bounced through so many areas and picked things up with such ease. If she'd stayed at anything, she'd have probably worked her way up to at least a senior leader position.

"What did you propose that was so new?" He pressed his lips to her cheek. He needed to touch her. Needed to remind himself that she was really here.

"A garden party."

He kept the chuckle contained. Because she was serious. "Umm…how is a garden party ground-breaking?"

"I never said my presentation was groundbreaking, just good. I *said* nothing after it was ground-breaking. So that means I won based on the silly metrics I made up in my head." She was practically glowing as she pulled away and found the wineglasses.

The ones from the unfinished toast. He swallowed as the memory boiled in his soul. They needed to discuss the ring she'd doodled, too. But he was not interrupting this.

Frankie poured wine into the glasses and passed him one.

He raised it and grinned. "To garden parties."

"Garden parties." Frankie clinked the glasses, took a heavy sip, then set the glass down. "I know it sounds silly, but I want to have the clients together. See how they mingle. See if there are any unexpected sparks or red flags."

"Oh." An event he'd have probably ditched when he was still a client. But that behavior was why Andilet had gone to such extremes with him. And he couldn't complain because the fake date they'd assigned him was standing barefoot in his kitchen.

"What is that *oh*?" Frankie tilted her head before setting the drink down.

"Nothing." He was not going to spoil the moment for her.

"No. It's something. Come on, spill." Frankie crossed her arms, ready for battle.

Decker set his wineglass down, "It's just that every society event I've been to has been stressful.

There are unspoken tensions and feuds. More than one fight has broken out. I just, I just don't know how much you'll learn. But I'm probably wrong."

He couldn't stand to see the frown on her lips. She was so excited about this.

"It will work." The words were soft, like she was trying to convince herself. "Plus Amelia already sent out the invite. It needs to be perfect." Frankie bit her lip. "Which means I will be working late some days for the next two weeks. I'll text you the schedule as soon as I know it."

"All right." Decker raised his glass and took a sip of the wine. He might work a few late nights then, too. If she was.

"And you'll come to the garden party? It's open to significant others. I want it to be a blend so it doesn't feel quite so much like a setup."

"I'll be there." He wasn't really fond of garden parties. But if Frankie wanted him there, then he'd eat some finger sandwiches and play croquet.

"How was your day?"

Decker smiled as she hopped up on the counter and grabbed a biscuit from the tin next to her. "I had a meeting today, too."

"Not the same." Frankie finished off the glass of wine and waved a hand when he held up the bottle to offer a refill. "I will need something besides a biscuit in my belly before I have another glass."

That was something he could handle. He grabbed

the dinner he'd put in the oven to keep warm. "How is my meeting not the same as yours?"

"Because you *always* have meetings." Frankie giggled. "I mean I do, too, but not fancy board-room meetings. What was your fancy boardroom meeting over? Jewelry?"

She did need something more than a biscuit in her belly. "You have anything for lunch?"

He was delaying the conversation. Delaying talking about the Francesca line. The new contract sitting on the table by the sofa. The one that had a bonus if Frankie came on as a full-time designer.

"No. The meeting ran over and then I had back-to-back client discussions. So your coffee and the tiny bag of almonds I found in my drawer are it."

"And now a glass of wine and biscuit. Go to the table. I will get you a plate." He watched as she jumped from the counter, mostly steady. One glass of wine wasn't a huge issue but when she had noth-ing else in her stomach…

He quickly put the stuffed peppers on the plate and hurried them out to her. She ate the food, then sat back in her chair.

"Your day. We got sidetracked." She let out a yawn. "Tell me about it."

She was exhausted. And if he were honest, Decker wasn't 100 percent sure how she'd react to the marketing decisions and requests for more items for the family she'd cursed before leaving here last time.

"It can wait. Just meetings."

Frankie raised an eyebrow and for a second he thought she planned to argue. Instead she grabbed her plate and his. "What do you say we drop these in the sink, vow to scrub them tomorrow, then go get dessert?"

"Dessert?" He wasn't really craving anything sweet but if she was, then he was all in. "Where do you want to go?"

Frankie put the dishes in the sink. She ran her tongue around her lips as she stepped up to him.

"I was thinking the bedroom." Her hands ran down his shirt. The scorching touch nearly brought him to his knees.

He grabbed her hand, lifting those beautiful, talented fingers to his lips. Decker pressed a kiss to each one, then scooped her up.

Frankie let out a little squeal, then wrapped her arms around his neck.

Decker grazed her lips with his. They had all night and he planned to spend most of it driving her to desire's edge. "I think the bedroom is the perfect place for dessert."

CHAPTER FIFTEEN

Won't be home until about ten thirty. Sorry.

DECKER LOOKED AT the phone and then back down at his draft table. He'd created more mock-ups this week than ever before. And Leona had looked at them and said she wanted another Francesca.

Except a Francesca line didn't exist. Technically.

Sure there was a contract for it. A request for twenty pieces with a price tag that had made his chief financial officer raise a brow until he heard *who* was asking for more pieces from Frankie. The problem was that the artist wasn't on board.

Because I haven't brought it up.

There never seemed to be a good time. She was focused on the party she was hosting this weekend. He didn't have any interest in the matchmaking function. But it was important to Frankie, so he always paid attention.

But it was lost on him how a garden party could be so important to Andilet's changing business model. And Decker was more than a little worried what would happen if Frankie didn't think it was successful.

He'd tried to recreate something close to the Francesca pieces Leona had seen. She'd spotted the difference immediately on each. He had to give it to the Pierces, they were experts in jewelry and designers.

The image on his board was a far cry from anything Frankie could draw up in minutes. And it was not going to work, either. He needed to ask her to sign the contract. Create the pieces that would sell for more money than she'd ever make at Andilet.

He let out a yawn and switched off his light. No sense hanging around here. He'd talk to Frankie tonight or, if she was too tired, tomorrow before they left for their respective offices.

That was their routine this week. Kiss goodnight. A brief conversation over coffee and then off to their offices.

Routines should feel nice. Should make him comfortable. They were settling back in.

But there was an undercurrent of tension. A floating fight just beneath the surface. Or maybe Decker was just expecting one.

He left the office and was at his flat without the travel time registering. Mental autopilot at its finest.

He pulled the contract out and set it on the kitchen table. They needed to discuss it tonight. Talk about the line. Talk about the name.

He personally liked keeping it Francesca—not because it was fancier. It would give Frankie some space between the brand and her chosen name. When her work was being worn by everyone, and it would be, then that space would matter.

Decker yawned again and looked at the clock, ten forty. He felt his lips turn down. He'd forgotten to update when he was running behind, but Frankie was usually either right on time or updated him. He looked at his phone and shook his head.

It was ten minutes. The tube might be delayed with no cell service. She might have left the office a little later. There were dozens of reasons she was a little late.

Ten minutes, Decker. Nothing to worry over.

But another ten passed. And then another.

He dialed her number but no answer. He left a message and then started for the door. Going... somewhere.

It wasn't like he could simply search her down.

He heard the key enter the lock and raced for the door, pulling it open, then standing there in shock. Frankie was on the threshold, holding his mother's shoulders.

"Decker?" His mother's voice was so faint. The way she said his name like a question more than a statement.

Tears coated the cheeks of both the women he loved.

"Hi, Mom. I wasn't expecting you."

"Is Harry here?" His mom looked past him but didn't step out of Frankie's hold.

"I already called Harry. He's on his way." Frankie rubbed his mother's shoulders. "Should be here any minute. Can we go inside Decker's flat?"

"Oh. Yes. Thank you, dear. This is—" Decker's mother looked at Frankie and pursed her lips.

"I'm Frankie. We met when I was walking here from the tube." Frankie looked at Decker, her eyes tearing up again, but she didn't remind his mother that they'd met a few weeks ago. And had dinner together a couple times after that.

Reminding his mother would only upset her, something the nursing staff had explained to his stepfather and him when the diagnosis came. The goal was redirection.

"And you know Decker." His mom walked in but looked around Decker's place with suspicion.

He followed her gaze. His place looked different. Frankie had put out some fluffy blankets she'd crocheted, and some stuffed animals. How she created them was beyond him. She could make them while having a conversation with him, never looking at the stuffy appearing in her hand.

"You decorated?" His mom laughed. "Not all white and gray." She held up a finger that was bonier than Decker had last seen it. "You have a woman living here. A woman making you happy."

"I do." His gaze met Frankie's. "Frankie."

His mom looked at Frankie, her scared and sad features brightening a bit. "You?"

"Me." Frankie winked at his mother as the door to the flat flew open.

"Honey." Harry walked up to Decker's mother and took her hand in his.

"Harry." She sank into his arms. "I don't know what happened. This nice lady…" She looked at Frankie and he could see her trying and failing to find the name Frankie had given her just a minute ago. She hesitated for a moment longer, then gave up.

"She brought me to Decker because they are in love and isn't that sweet."

Frankie slipped to Decker's side and wrapped an arm around his waist as she leaned her head against his shoulder.

"Very." Harry looked at Decker. "Sorry. She doesn't usually sundown but today was rough, and then when it started getting darker, she was agitated. She went to bed and I took a long shower trying to relax and the next thing I know Frankie is ringing my line over and over again."

"Harry—"

"We'll discuss it more tomorrow, Decker." Harry looked at his mother and kissed her forehead. The dementia was moving faster now. It would be time for tough discussions before long.

Decker looked at Frankie. He'd waited too long

to find a love that his mother would remember. That dream was gone.

If I hadn't waited, I wouldn't have Frankie.

That provided some balm. But knowing he was letting his mom down was a bitter pill.

She doesn't remember that I am letting her down.

Decker bit the inside of his cheek as that terrible thought radiated through him. A shattered dream was still a dream, even if the person you loved didn't realize it.

At least he'd put his father's empire back together.

"I am going to take her home. And get some rest." Harry ran his hand over his wife's. "Good night, Decker and Frankie."

"Night," they managed at the same time.

Frankie rubbed his arm, then followed Harry and his mother to the door and locked it behind them. "Want to talk about it?"

"No." Decker shook his head. There was nothing to discuss. Not yet, anyway. When Harry was ready, Decker would make sure his mother had the best care available. Until then, he'd focus on what he could control.

"But we do need to talk." Decker moved to the counter where he'd put the contract. This wasn't the best time. But they needed it filed and ready for when Mrs. Pierce was ready to have a meeting.

Frankie tilted her head as she walked toward

him. "What is that? A contract?" She halted and shook her head. "Decker, it's been a long day."

"I know. I've actually had it for several days but you've been busy and the clients are interested in the line and the name is still Francesca instead of Frankie. I know that is a sticking point but I think it is good because it will give you distance from the line when it explodes, and it is going to explode."

Frankie held up her hand. "Take a breath."

Decker followed the command, mostly because he'd spat out so many words with no break that his lungs were screaming. "I had a whole speech planned out and there was never a good time. I know I bungled it. I know—"

Frankie's finger was over his lips. "It's all right. How many pieces?"

There was an air in the question. A looseness that sent a bead of worry to his soul. They were both tired. Long weeks at the office and then to-night had drained everything.

"This one doesn't specify. It is a flat rate per piece for everything in the line for the next three years. And a bonus if—"

"Three years?" Frankie interrupted as she looked at the contract, then at him. "What if I sign that and in three years we aren't…?" She blew out a breath. "What if this…?" She didn't complete that sentence, either, but it was easy to decode the hesitation.

"Frankie." He set the contract down. "We are going to be together. We are." He pressed his lips to each cheek, then grazed them over her lips. "I love you."

"I know." Frankie's gaze darted to the contract. "I know." She stepped out of his arms, grabbed the pen next to the contract and flipped to the final page. She signed each place where his assistant had placed a sticky note requesting her signature.

"Don't you want to read it?"

"No." Frankie put the cap back on the pen. "Right now I want to go to bed. Tomorrow is a new day."

He looked at her flowy signature but the happiness he'd expected from it didn't materialize.

It was just the long day. Just the unexpected interruption tonight. The realization that he'd never achieve the dream for his mother understandably souring things.

That was all.

It was.

Frankie dropped three designs on the entry table and frowned as she headed for their bedroom. This was the second night that she'd returned to the flat late only to find that Decker was still at the office. It was like he was doubling down on the jewelry business.

Or is it that I'm gone most evenings so he's taking advantage of the opportunity to get more done.

Still, there was that grim determination in him. A steel hardened in the fires of other's dreams. She couldn't help but wonder if Decker knew what he really wanted.

He'd told her on one of their fake dates that he wasn't sure what he'd be doing if he hadn't chased down his father's dream; that their dreams were intertwined.

And his mother's dream... Tears floated in Frankie's eyes. Decker's mother was sweet and Frankie wished she'd known the woman before her diagnosis took a darker turn, but the truth was Decker was never going to achieve that dream.

When he married, if he married, Harry would stand there as his family, capturing all the memories his mother could no longer hold.

Frankie looked at her watch and sighed as she pulled out her phone.

Heading to bed. Exhausted. Don't stay at the office much longer, okay.

Okay. Love you.

At least his texts were popping back quickly. He never ignored one. Never left it on read.

But that didn't mean it wasn't lonely heading to bed on her own.

It would change when he knew she wasn't staying late, too. It would.

It had to.

Her brain's rationality did not ease her heart's concerns.

* * *

So far two fights had broken out. Not fistfights but low discussions and cutting looks that separated people into two clear sides. That was a wrinkle Frankie had not anticipated. However, it had taught her a lot. And three women had stepped up to let her know one of the male guests had a reputation for slipping things into dates' drinks. A fact his father had paid the authorities to lose interest in.

There were certainly individuals they shouldn't put together. And a woman and two men who should be dropped from their client list immediately. But this was far from the successful event she'd hyped it up to be. The only thing keeping it together at all was that no one wanted it to slip into the gossip mills that they'd gotten into a public row at a matchmaking garden party.

Decker had been right. This was not a success story. He might have earned the right to gloat, if he'd showed up. The text had arrived ten minutes before the party was supposed to kick off.

Stuck in meeting.

No *I'll be late*. No *Sorry*. Just a note to indicate that something more important than Frankie had taken precedence.

If his mother wasn't declining, would he even come out of the office long enough to care about someone else?

That was a thought for some other time. Right

now Frankie needed to focus on saving this train wreck.

She bit the inside of her cheek as she listened to a polite untitled aristocrat discuss his horses. The man was sweet and there was a woman Frankie had met with, who'd chosen not to attend, who'd match with him perfectly.

One tiny success in a business she was starting to think was on its way out. At least the way Andilet ran it. People weren't interested in social marriages anymore. The polite term sounded better than arranged marriage or contractual agreement, but it was still the case.

People wanted more. And they deserved more. But that meant "success" for Andilet had to look different. It couldn't mean a serious partnership or marriage. It had to mean... Well, she wasn't sure what it had to mean, but this business model was flailing.

"Think we should call it?" Amelia strode up next to her as the horse enthusiast walked away. The smile on her face hardly masking her frustration.

"Probably. I think social decorum is the only thing keeping some of them from using the croquet mallets on each other." Frankie let out a sigh. "I'm sorry, Amelia."

"Not the first time we've tried something and had it go sideways. We learned several things, though, and I think I know exactly who to set Eddie up with."

"Tess, right. The two of them will talk horses all night." Frankie felt a little weight slip off her shoulders. "A few people have already taken their leave. How do we get the others to take the hint?" This was already a disaster; she didn't want to make it worse.

"Let me handle it. You start cleaning. I find routine helps clear the mind." Amelia didn't wait for any response as she wandered off.

Frankie took the cue and picked up some uneaten desserts and headed for the staging area they'd set up in the venue Andilet had rented for this disaster. Amelia was right; it was nice to have something monotonous to do.

Unfortunately it let her mind focus too much on the fact that the man she loved was unavailable for the one thing she'd asked him to attend. A meeting took precedence over her.

Again.

He was living his life for ghosts. One long gone and one whose disease was robbing them of their last years. How was she to compete with that?

I can't.

"Amelia told me I'd find you here. I thought the party went for another forty-five?"

Frankie didn't bother to hide the tears when she looked up at him. "You were right. This wasn't the best idea, so we ended it early."

"The good news is your Francesca line sold multiple designs today. You don't need this." Decker took a step toward her but she stepped back.

"Yes, I do." How could he not understand this? "I need this. I need to do this on my own, Decker." Frankie's chest was caving in. This wasn't the time or place, but if she waited, she worried she'd lose every last bit of willpower. "This is mine."

"No. This is a job you took because you needed one and they sent you on a fake date with their worst client to trick him." He pinched his lips. "I didn't mean that."

"You did." Frankie shrugged her shoulders. "The worst part is I can't say you're wrong. This isn't my dream. But you're just like my parents."

His cheeks colored. "That is not fair."

"It is. As long as I am working on the Francesca line. As long as there are designs coming in, then you are happy. But you're rooting against what I want. You said this party might be a disaster."

"And it was!" Decker pushed his hand through his hair and pointed to the closed door—through which anyone outside would be able to hear their row. "It's ended early, and from what I briefly gathered, there was more than one argument."

Three—if you counted this one.

"But you want me to leave Andilet, want me to work for Heughs full-time, right?"

"You are a natural, Frankie! Your raw design talent is going to waste here."

"So you want it going to your father's dream?"

Her words hit their target perfectly. Now he was the one stepping back. "You are living other people's lives. Other people's dreams."

"And you are living your life in spite of others. Letting your parents dictate what careers matter rather than chasing your dreams!" Decker crossed his arms. "You have a gift others would kill for. They spend years perfecting a craft and never getting as good as your doodles, and you are throwing it away because you have some misguided belief that those gifts aren't worth anything. I've tried to show just how much they are worth."

"To benefit you." Frankie hated to hear herself lashing out. Hated how true the echoes of Decker's words sounded. "I'll send someone to pick up my things."

The words were out; there was no taking them back.

"Fine." Decker shook his head. "Fine." He opened his mouth but no other words came out. He turned and walked out.

CHAPTER SIXTEEN

DECKER HAD GOTTEN UP, drunk coffee and gone to the office for the last three days. That was all he'd managed.

Frankie's stuff was still here. She'd said she'd send someone to pick it up. He could send it to her, but the idea of packing it up... The rhythm of putting it into boxes and bags. The acknowledgment that when it left, there was no reason for her to ever return. Decker hadn't been able to do it.

A knock at the door sent his stomach into a spin. He wasn't optimistic enough to think it was Frankie. But if it was someone who'd come to collect her things...that would destroy him.

The knock came again and he forced his feet to move. He had to be at the office in an hour. Meet with Leona and sort out their requests for the exclusive Francesca line.

Francesca. Frankie.

His body ached but he didn't stop. He swung the door open and was stunned to see his mother. Clear-eyed. A cup-holder with three coffees and a bag of muffins.

"Before you ask, Harry is downstairs. I wanted to have a quick chat, while I am fully myself." His mother's smile was sad but her shoulders were straight.

"Is Frankie here?" She looked around the apartment. "I wasn't sure what kind of coffee to get her. Harry suggested iced. Said she looks like an iced coffee gal."

"She is a coffee kind of gal. Ice, hot, latte, mocha. All of it." The words were rough as they fell from his lips. "But she isn't here."

His mother set the coffees on the table by the door, the one Frankie always dropped her purse on. "She's very nice."

Decker couldn't do more than nod.

"But she deserves to be loved for herself." His mother put a hand on his cheek. "Fully."

"I do." He saw so much of Frankie's potential. Saw what could make her happy.

"Your father loved me, too." His mother grabbed one of the coffees and passed it to him, then took one for herself. "You were too young to remember. There were so many good days. But in the end, he loved Heughs more. The company was his life. When I worked for him, I was in his orbit. When I stepped back, it was like I was disappointing him."

She moved around Decker and took a seat on the sofa, fingering one of the colorful blankets. "But that's not what I'm here for. I'm moving into a memory care facility."

"Mom."

"No arguing. Harry isn't taking it well, though he is trying to put on a happy mask for me. I want to make the choice. The day is coming when I don't get to make it. When all my choices are gone. But this is one that he is terribly sad about, but will support. Because that is what Harry does. He supports me. So *you* are going to support him."

Decker swallowed all the arguments he wanted to make. The platitudes that they still had time. His mom was right; this was what was best. It gave her some dignity from a disease intent on robbing her of everything.

But that didn't mean it didn't hurt.

"I hate this." He put his arms around her.

"Me, too. But we are at the place where there are no good choices, Decker. Just a cascade of bad ones." She kissed his cheek and sat back. "I am so proud of you. So proud."

"Not hurt that you might not see me walk down the aisle? I'm not letting you down?" That question wasn't meant to slip from his lips. It was selfish. This moment wasn't about him.

"Decker, I want you happy. Whatever that means to you." She paused and took a deep breath. "Life is lived for yourself, not for others. I am hurt that there will be moments I miss, even if I am still here. But none of that is your journey, only you get to decide your path."

That was what Frankie had been trying to get

through to him. What she'd pressed on him on the fake dates and the real ones. The worry she'd had over his fixation on her designs.

He'd actively tried to promote design over the job she had. The one that wasn't her dream, but that was hers. Yes, he'd suspected the garden party would be a bust, but rather than be there to support her, no matter the outcome, he'd stayed to work on something at Heughs.

Demonstrating, once and for all, where his priorities lay. No wonder she'd told him off. He deserved far worse.

"I have a meeting, but I support you, Mom. And I am going to do everything possible to make sure Frankie knows that nothing is coming before her again—assuming she forgives me."

"I hope she does." His mother grabbed her coffee and stood. A morning of hard truths did not leave room for platitudes. Frankie would forgive him or she wouldn't.

Either way he needed her to know that he believed in her. No matter what career she was chasing.

Frankie had called out of work, again.

She looked around her small flat. With the amount of money in her account, she could start looking for a larger place. Maybe a two bedroom where she could make an office.

She still hadn't gone to pick up her stuff or asked

one of her friends to do it. Something about that finality was out of reach right now. She'd get around to it.

Just like she'd get around to returning to work. Amelia had been so easygoing about the garden party failure. She'd texted Frankie to remind her that some ideas bombed even when they seemed perfect.

Frankie suspected she was a little happy one of Frankie's golden ideas was actually brass.

Standing up, she paced the flat. Ever since the breakup, all she seemed to do was fidget. That and design. She'd drafted three dresses, a purse and five pieces of jewelry.

All moody pieces for shoppers stuck in their feelings. At least that was what Frankie was telling herself. The truth was that the artist was deep in her feelings.

Two sharp raps echoed on her door.

Frankie slowly slid past the bed. She wasn't expecting anyone and Decker never knocked in such a demanding way.

Maybe it was someone delivering her stuff.

Decker would certainly be within his rights to send her stuff back to her. They'd parted so publicly, with such hurtful words. She'd been angry. Justifiably, but part of her wondered if she'd overreacted.

I didn't. Not really.

The words had been honest but saying them in

the cleaning area of the garden party, with raised voices, was less than ideal. That was a choice she'd regret forever.

The handle was cold as she counted to three, then forced herself to open the door.

"Catalina?"

Her sister burst in without even a hello.

"So this is your place? Cute." Her sister squeezed her eyes shut but that didn't stop the tears leaking out the sides.

"What's going on?"

"I stopped at your office, but they said you'd called in. I figured you were here playing hooky, just like the old days. Not that you ever invited me."

"To play hooky or to my place?" Frankie was having a pout, she knew that, but she and her sister had always talked through jibs and taunts rather than address their unspoken rivalry.

"Both." Catalina flopped on the bed. "I always wanted to play hooky. Skip a day or week or whatever. Walk away."

Whatever Frankie had expected it wasn't that. "I'll make some tea."

"Mom and Dad are disappointed in me." Catalina stifled a sob. "I guess they told their colleagues about my promotion and they're concerned about walking it back."

Frankie gripped the handle of the kettle so hard

just to keep from throwing it against the wall as the anger those words caused radiated through her.

"How bloody dare they!" She started the kettle and stepped out to see her sister. "You got unfairly shafted at the hospital; this is not about them. Period."

"How is it so easy for you?" Catalina took a tissue out of the box that Frankie had used when her tears over Decker had threatened to drown her.

"Easy? Please."

"No. I mean it. I've always been jealous of your ability to just drown them out. To do whatever you want. To fly away on some new adventure. Some new job. New life. No worries over what our parents say. Just choosing you."

Frankie's flat was small but that didn't explain why she couldn't get enough air in her lungs. "What?"

"Don't make me explain it again." Catalina let out a sob and grabbed another tissue. "Just tell me how you get to the point you don't care. I mean, even your nickname. Frankie. They hate it and you've never cared."

It was like she was seeing Catalina for the first time. "Do you not like your name?" There were other things they needed to discuss. But this was important.

"I'm named after a dead queen our mother is obsessed with." Catalina let out a laugh but there was no humor in it. "I prefer Cat, always have, but when she hears it…" Her sister flinched and brushed another tear away.

"All right, Cat." Her sister's smile hearing the name lit up the small room. "The answer is I do care. I care a lot."

Frankie's gaze fell on the designs. The ones that she'd come up with when she was tired and frustrated and in the pits of despair. They were good. Really good.

That was what she wanted and she'd run from it because it wasn't enough. But Cat had done everything asked of her. Everything. And it wasn't enough.

They were never going to be enough. Decker was right. She was Flyaway Frankie to spite her family. Not because she truly lacked commitment. It was a rebellion and one that was only damaging her.

She sat beside her sister and outlined her history of running, held her hand while Cat cried about the promotion and the fact that they were failures in their parents' eyes.

"So these are the designs you talked about." Cat looked over the sketches. "I don't know anything about design. I live my life in scrubs but I love this necklace." She pointed to the little broken heart with a key dangling farther down the chain.

"I'll make sure you get the first one off the line." As she said the words, Frankie knew her life was changing. She was going to quit Andilet. Work for

Heughs and look at starting her own fashion line. No. She *was* starting her own fashion line.

"Off the line?" Cat looked at the necklace.

"I work freelance for a jewelry line and I'm starting my own company. It might take me time but I am doing it. Mom and Dad will never approve of us. But they don't get to control our lives. We make our choices."

"You make it sound so easy." Cat stood and looked at her watch. "I have a shift. I appreciate this."

"Anytime." Frankie meant it. "And it's not easy. But it's worth it."

Now it was time to chase her dreams. She was too talented to worry about her family's expectations.

And, as soon as she dropped her notice at the office, she was finding Decker.

CHAPTER SEVENTEEN

DECKER LOOKED AT the clock on his wall and shook his head. They were late. Again.

Because my time is theirs.

They'd financed his first business. Made all this possible.

But that loan was paid long ago.

His father had lost his business but Decker's accounts were healthy. More than healthy.

But what if...?

Decker mentally shut that thought off. Worrying over the business was the thing that kept him here when he should be finding Frankie. This was the reason she'd been so right to point out the issues.

Even after talking to his mother, he'd come here. Not canceled the meeting. Not rescheduled it.

This stopped now. Period.

"Miranda." Decker looked at his watch. "I am heading out. Please reach out to Leona Pierce's assistant and let them know she needs to reschedule."

Miranda's face lit up. "Oh, they're going to hate that."

"Then why do you look so excited?" Decker grabbed his phone.

"Because I've wanted to do this for years!" His assistant's laugh was far too close to diabolical for comfort but at least it wasn't directed at him. "They've kept us waiting so many times. It's ridiculous."

"Yes. And it ends now. I do apologize for not nipping it sooner." His obsession had hurt himself, his workforce and Frankie. No more.

He waved as he headed to the door and down the lift. He was almost to the front door when Leona walked in. The older woman's white hair was coifed and she looked unperturbed by the late hour. Her husband was talking on his phone, not bothering to make eye contact with anyone his wife had kept waiting.

"Decker, front door service. I like it." Leona held her hand out.

Decker took it, briefly. His stomach tightened. This was the moment. The change.

Something ended here.

His obsessive tie to this place...or any hope of a relationship with Frankie.

"I'm sorry. I have another appointment."

Mrs. Pierce took off her oversized sunglasses. "I am sure they won't mind waiting."

Decker shook his head. "I appreciate everything you did for me in the early days of Heughs Jewelry and your business, but from now on, if you are more than ten minutes late for your appointment, you will not be guaranteed an appointment that day. It is our standard policy."

Leona's cheeks heated but it was hardly shame crossing her porcelain features. "We can always take our business elsewhere."

"You can." Decker shrugged despite the tension pouring through him. Standing up here and now was hard but necessary. "I would hate to lose you as clients, but you can. And of course we could cancel any of your current orders."

"The Francesca line items—"

"Can go to someone else. I have no doubt the pieces will sell, you need not worry. We will return the deposits."

"No." Leona put her glasses back on her face. "Those are mine." She stormed off, but before they were out of the office, her husband turned and gave Decker a small nod.

The lightness in his shoulders was long overdue. As was finding Frankie.

Frankie's hand was aching and her back was screaming at her but she was not getting up from the design chair until she finished this logo. Or at least had one that wasn't completely terrible. The floor was littered with tossed pieces of paper.

Hell, she'd even tried the digital format she loved and given up after version two. Her preferred medium just didn't flow for logos.

Neither does paper.

She had a plan. A way to show her intent to Decker. But it only worked if there was a logo here.

Looking at her watch, she let out a sigh. It was only three o'clock. She had plenty of time.

Amelia hadn't tried very hard to talk her into staying at Andilet. She'd told Frankie she was a good dating coach. But that she wasn't sure it was marketable long-term.

Which was translation for the garden party was the last attempt Andilet was making at change. Frankie thought that was the wrong move, but it wasn't her business. Not her concern. Though if Patricia decided she wanted a new position, Frankie would hire her as soon as she could afford to take on employees.

She stared at the design on the paper and let out a growl. Why did nothing work? She crumpled the paper and tossed it with the dozens of others.

"Should I be worried to find you in the design room with—" Decker's eyes widened as he stared at the debris "—paper covering the floor?"

Frankie stood, the urge to rush to him running through her, but there were things to say first.

"Decker, why are you here?" He was early. Far too early. He shouldn't be back for hours still.

"I live here. And I'm hoping that you do, too." Decker swallowed. "I am so sorry, Frankie. I should have been at the garden party. I should have focused on what you want for yourself."

"I quit." Frankie bit her lip and grabbed the piece of paper closest to her feet. She unraveled it and stuck her tongue out. "It's a terrible logo design." She turned it around. "But you were right. What I want is to design, not just for Heughs. I'll still do jewelry but I want clothing, too. Sustainable fashion lines that are affordable."

This was her dream. Hers. What she wanted. The life she chose for herself.

"You are going to be the top designer in London. We're going to travel the world for fashion shows."

"We? You'll come with me?" She wanted him there. Wanted him by her side whenever possible.

"Every time you want me to. My business can run itself without me when it needs to and video teleconferencing is always an option. I'm sorry I lashed out, too. You were right. I was living another's dream."

"Decker."

"I made changes today, too. First, no client gets to be more than ten minutes late. Second, unless it is absolutely necessary, I leave at six. We have a life outside the office. I love you. That is my dream and I am not willing to bend. I even sent Leona Pierce packing today when she and her husband were late."

"You did?" She knew what that would have taken. "That must have been hard."

"I suspect it was as hard as coming here and drawing up logos. We've both let others' expectations chase us." Decker opened his arms and she stepped into them.

Her soul sighed as she laid her head against his shoulder. This was where she was meant to be.

EPILOGUE

FRANKIE ROLLED THE design around on the tablet and sighed. She'd uploaded the final drawing last night. This morning she was taking one last look to see if there was anything to add.

But it was perfect. Hopefully the bride liked it.

"That the final product?" Decker looked over her shoulder, then kissed her cheek.

They'd worked together for the last year. Her fashion house was in a few small shows next spring. All financed by the Francesca line. Decker was right, the line was now the top seller for Heughs.

And he'd been by her side the whole time. They were a team. Cheering each other on with each success and holding each other when setbacks arose.

"It is." She turned the ring on the tablet. "You said the groom asked for something unique. Something that would stand out on her hand."

"I did."

"I'm almost sorry to see this one go." Frankie smiled at the design. "This one is perfect." She'd never felt that way about a product. Oh, she liked her designs, but this one…

Decker had been so specific on what the groom had ordered but left leeway for her creative freedom.

"Really?" His breath was warm on her ear and his thumb rubbed her stomach as he held her.

"Yes, really." She pressed her lips to his. "Weird, huh?"

"I think it's quite fortuitous, actually."

"Look at you pulling out the big words." Frankie pushed her backside into him.

"Yes." Decker took the tablet and set it down. "I am pulling out the big words, because I wasn't sure how to get this ring designed."

"What?" Frankie looked at him, then back at the ring. "Decker?" She hadn't designed her own ring, had she? But as she saw the smile grow on his face, Frankie jumped into his arms. "Yes. Yes. A million times yes."

"I haven't asked anything." His lips captured hers, then he pulled back. "And the ring isn't made."

"I don't care. Ask now." Frankie cupped the sides of his cheek.

"Will you marry me, Frankie?"

"Yes!" She sighed. "But I want to rush this order."

"Really?" Decker ran his hand along her chin. "I thought you hated rush orders."

"Not when I'm the bride."

* * * * *

If you enjoyed this story,
check out these other great reads from
Juliette Hyland

Beauty and the Brooding CEO
Fake Dating the Vet
How to Tame a King
How to Win a Prince

All available now!

Harlequin® Reader Service

Enjoyed your book?

Try the perfect subscription for Romance readers and get more great books like this delivered right to your door.

See why over 10+ million readers have tried Harlequin Reader Service.

Start with a Free Welcome Collection with free books and a gift—valued over $20.

Choose any series in print or ebook. See website for details and order today:

TryReaderService.com/subscriptions